"What do you see when you look at the target?" Her father had always asked the same question.

"I look at the target, then the sights."

One time, though, he asked, "What do you see right before you look at the sights and pull the trigger?"

She grinned, knowing the answer. "I look at the gaps between the sights and the target." She explained his instructions back to him. "To make sure they're even."

"How big is the gap?"

She held herself very still, the target pistol steady in her twelve-year-old's grip. "It's big," she said slowly. She frowned, doubting her answer. "Right before I pull the trigger, it's all I see." She turned to him, expecting correction.

His thoughtful frown matched hers. "That's right," he said. "That's just how I would say it." He had gripped her shoulder. "If you don't see the gap, don't pull the trigger. But when the gap is all you see, you're dead on."

About the Author

Lisa Shapiro lives in Portsmouth, New Hampshire. She is the author of *The Color of Winter* (Naiad, 1996). Her short stories appear in the Naiad anthologies *Dancing in the Dark* and *Lady Be Good*.

SEA
to shining
SEA

BY
LISA SHAPIRO

THE NAIAD PRESS, INC.
1997

Printed in the United States of America on acid-free paper
First Edition

Editor: Christine Cassidy
Cover designer: Bonnie Liss (Phoenix Graphics)
Typesetter: Sandi Stancil

Library of Congress Cataloging-in-Publication Data

Shapiro, Lisa. 1962 –
    Sea to shining sea / Lisa Shapiro.
        p.   cm.
    ISBN 1-56280-177-5 (alk. paper)
    I. Title.
PS3569.H34146S4   1997
813'.54—dc21   97-10803
                                                                        CIP

*For Lynne, who calms the torrent,
and the Shapiros — Sandy, Nicki, Beth, Jeff
and Grandma Sarah.*

Acknowledgments

There are a number of gracious, intelligent individuals whose expertise helped shape this story.

I would like to thank John T. Wilson, engineer, inventor and superb marksman, who taught me to handle guns safely and let me wear his holster — a true friend. I am in the debt of Special Agent Peter S. Ginieres, and Special Agent John C. Huyler, of the FBI's Boston Field Office — these men have my respect and gratitude. I must also acknowledge Ray Coulombe, the font of knowledge in the New Hampshire mountains; Beth Jefferson, of Liberty Mutual, who shared computer magic and the romance of sailing; Susannah Colt, Esq., premiere source of lesbian legal information; Lis Anderson, the smartest nurse I know; Patricia Bennett, of Trussell & Bennett Financial Services, Inc.; and the incomparable reference librarians at the Portsmouth, New Hampshire Public Library.

My thanks also to Mika Meadows, confidante and intrepid traveling companion; Martha Morrison, an artist who reads between the lines; and Roberta Soar, reader.

Special thanks to Christine Cassidy for her beautiful sense of timing and character development.

There is one other person to whom I owe acknowledgment. Her assistance is unparalleled, her strength and patience without measure. For the peace, beauty and simplicity we share, my loving thanks to my life partner, Lynne D'Orsay.

SEA
to shining
SEA

Fidelity, Bravery, and Integrity

FBI Motto

Prologue

She knew the feel of the brick. Pressed against it, her palms tingled and her face burned. She clutched the wall but it was unrelenting. It offered no assistance, no escape. She kicked backward. For an intimate moment, she knew the solid impact of bone. His weight eased and she turned. Under the streetlight, malice and mist distorted his features. Rain dripped, saturated with a rotten-garbage smell. She watched as droplets beaded on his brow and upper lip. Her body heat evaporated. For a silent, enduring time, there was only his breath and hers, mingled like wraiths between them.

She surged toward the street. For one hope-filled instant, she thought she'd broken free. He barked, a humanless grunt, and his mauling hands trapped her. Pinned against the brick, her head bounced dully. Distantly, she heard it thud. Finally, she cried out, and his glove-toughened palm hit her mouth. Like a boxer, he slammed her solar plexus. Air left her lungs.

The wall couldn't hold her; she folded to the damp cement. She had no air, only a sickening dread. Her ribs heaved but sucked nothing. The gloved fist hung in her vision. He broke her nose. She closed her eyes. She had no sight, no breath. Panic scratched. No sound. There was only the taste of the blood that choked her, only the press of pain as he raped her.

Part I
JUNE GAVIN

Chapter 1

"He's gonna push her."

"Is that what he said?"

"Hell, yeah. Uh, yes, ma'am. He's been screaming about pushing her off for two hours. Here." The trooper shoved a megaphone into her hands. "Get him down. It's almost rush hour."

The interstate bridge was closed in both directions. At seven a.m., the traffic, still light, had been re-routed. A quarter-mile distant, one of the smaller drawbridges was up, and a ship, flanked by chugging tugs, was making headway up-river. From her vantage point, June could see the towns on both sides, one in New Hampshire, one in Maine. And in the middle, a disheveled man with a death-grip on his girlfriend.

June looked down. Coast Guard boats had motored into position. From this height, the water would feel like brick.

She asked, "How strong is the current?"

The trooper pointed to the drawbridge. "Last year, a guy was trying to outrun a drug bust and he gate-crashed the barrier while the bridge was going up. It took a team of divers four days to find his body. The current dragged the car a mile out to sea."

Wet-suited Coast Guard divers stood ready. The cargo ship had halted; the tugs jockeyed and bobbed. Motorists, stalled at the drawbridge, waited in line.

June surveyed the interstate bridge. In the north-bound lane, New Hampshire state troopers, bulky in their green uniforms, stood behind patrol cars. Maine troopers, facing south and wearing blue, had amassed a similar force. They looked like squads of opposing linebackers. Car doors open, radios turned up, light bars strobing, they wanted action. A SWAT team from one of the local forces crouched behind the lane dividers.

"Agent Gavin?" The young agent looked like his necktie was choking him. "We were serving an arrest warrant for eighty-five thousand in unpaid child support. The ex-wife lives in Rochester. The girl-friend's from Dover."

"What does he want?"

"We, uh, haven't established productive communication."

"Did Boston send a man yet?" The booming voice had a familiar ring. June turned. "Hey, sure-shot."

"Hi, Bass."

"You the negotiator? Get this clown down for me. It's all I can do to keep SWAT from tackling both of them over the side."

"Tell tactical to move back, and clear those troopers out. I want this lane empty. And get me cell phones. I'm not going to yell at this guy." She handed the megaphone to the rookie. "Do it." He straightened so fast his back popped. He rushed off.

"Kid needs to slow down." Bass Deacon grinned. "I thought you were still hiding under a desk at Washington Metro."

"You got a gut on you, Bass. I asked for Boston."

"Took you long enough. Boston's a good office. What squad?"

"Violent crimes."

He grunted. "About time. Wasted talent, putting you behind a desk."

"Employee assistance was good experience." He didn't answer. They both knew it was a lie. He'd been close to the mark to say she'd been hiding.

Bass Deacon had been her firearms training instructor at Quantico. He'd recruited her off a competitive shooting range. At the time, she'd just finished graduate school, and she'd just won first place in regional free pistol.

* * * * *

7

"An M.S.W.," Bass had mused. "Social work's interesting. But I really need a sharpshooter." Both walls of his tiny office were covered with mounted trophy fish, the origin of his nickname. From the award plaques and framed certificates, she learned that his real name was Beauregard. "The High Standard Olympic isn't a bad target pistol."

"Yes, sir." Her competition gun, with a six-and-three-quarter-inch tapered barrel and micro-adjustable rear sights, had been a gift from her father. She'd been winning at free pistol since she was twelve.

Bass held up a gun. "The Olympic's a little light for a service weapon. This is a nine millimeter single-action Browning High Power. It's accurate enough to hold one inch at thirty yards."

"Single action?"

"Our hostage rescue team carries it condition one. Cocked and locked, and one up the spout." He ejected the ammunition clip and set the gun on his desk. "Some firearms instructors think it's unsafe, but it just takes a little training."

She didn't hesitate. She picked up the handgun and pulled back the slide, checking to see that the chamber was empty. She inserted the magazine and charged the slide to load a round. Then she ejected the magazine. With one round locked in the chamber, the clip had room for an extra cartridge. She looked at him expectantly. As he handed it to her, their eyes met. She slapped the full clip into the gun and her thumb engaged the safety.

He nodded. "Right so far. Let's go down to the range."

A dozen curious field agents and a handful of

instructors joined them, hands shoved into windbreaker pockets.

"What's with the one-hand grip," someone scoffed.

She adjusted her ear protectors. She used one hand to aim her pistol, rather than the two-handed isometric grip favored by academy instructors. For target shooting, the increased field-depth was an advantage.

She sighted along the Browning's steel-mounted sights, measuring the tiny gaps to either side of the front blade. For a second, she focused on the black dot of the bull's-eye, then pulled her focus back to the space between her sights. There was a small gap between the edge of the front sight and the circular edge of the target. When the gap filled her vision, when it was all she saw, she squeezed the trigger. Successive rounds disappeared into the target's black center.

She loaded a fresh magazine and cocked the gun, then moved to a different part of the range. The metal plates were too easy to hit. It was a course designed to test speed. She doubled her distance from the mark, took her time and dropped every plate. Once more, she reloaded. Before she engaged the safety, she cocked the gun.

Bass Deacon couldn't stop chuckling. He'd turned to the quiet group and said, "I think we've got a new sniper."

June looked at the man she'd trained with for six years. "What are you doing in New Hampshire?"

"Trying to retire. They sent me to Budapest to teach at the international academy. I got a commendation, and when I got back, Brenda had split. I asked them to please transfer my ass out of Virginia. So they made me supervisory senior."

"That sounds tough."

"Yeah. Why'd you pick Boston?"

"I thought I didn't know anyone in New England."

She'd forgotten how much she enjoyed his laugh. "You're too good to hide. Who's your supervisor?" he asked.

"Shane Isaacs."

"I'll give him a call."

She sighed. In a matter of days, everyone in the field office would be calling her "sure-shot." Bureau agents were a tight-knit bunch of bastards.

The rookie agent returned. Grumbling troopers had cleared the bridge, and the deadbeat dad, still clutching his hostage, was inching his way toward the phone that had been placed within reach. June activated her phone.

Bass slapped her on the back. "Okay, Gavin. Go to work."

She hadn't heard those words in a long time.

Chapter Two

Government Center's red brick plaza was awash in May sunlight. Scraggly tulips, in a sunken trough, looked entombed. Architects, trying for a tiered effect, had over-emphasized city hall. The blocky edifice encroached like an overbite. Behind it, the elegant old statehouse sat arm-in-arm with a visitor center.

The streets in downtown Boston were so narrow that buildings seemed to lean, like glass-and-concrete conferees touching heads. Alone on its island plaza, the John F. Kennedy Federal Building stood straight.

Across the street, in a building shaped like a

croissant, were the private offices of the FBI. A copy center and travel agency shared the ground level. Above them were two floors of lawyers, and on the uppermost level, the county trial court. Taking up four floors in the middle, and responsible for a territory that covered four states, was the Boston field office.

Special Agent June Gavin hit the revolving doors shoulder first. In the public lobby, modern art adorned one wall; a standing directory opposed the elevators. Among the business set, heavy make-up was back for the women, power ties a thing of the past for men. Her heels were lower, but she stood inches taller than the other women. In creased slacks and a sports jacket, she might have been discounted, except for her size. She stood six feet even in flats. Leather pumps gave her an extra inch.

Visitors heading for Bureau reception departed at level six. June rode to the seventh floor. Two cameras, suspended from the hall's low ceiling, watched as she keyed a number into the computerized pad. Each agent used a private code. The latch released, and June followed the corridor.

To date, a dozen years with the Bureau had earned her a commendation for valor and the right to choose her field office of preference. The bravery, she feared, was a fluke, not so much an accident of circumstance as of inspiration. A moment of genius she might be called upon to repeat, like the stories that followed her through the hallways ... *the shot, the shot, the shot.* The words backed her up against a wall of doubt.

"I'm afraid I couldn't do it again."

She'd said it during a debriefing. Her supervisor

took the comment for humility. As far as other agents were concerned, she had nothing left to prove. She'd succeeded on a mission and therefore would always succeed. Only June seemed to understand that success required a balancing measure of failure, that the cost of the impossible might someday have to be repaid.

A few eyebrows had raised when she'd requested a transfer from Quantico's hostage rescue team. But time passed. Eyesight, everyone assumed, dimmed with age. If they'd bothered to retest her eyes, they might have pressed for a different explanation. Her shooting was as sharp as ever.

"Hands steady. Inhale. Breathe half-way out. Now hold it. Squeeze the trigger. That's my girl. Good shot."

She couldn't forget her father's instructions. Shooting with him was one of her earliest memories.

Finally, in an interview room, she settled on a reason. "I'd like to use my degree."

File pages flipped. "Masters in Social Work. Employee assistance is big right now."

She didn't even have to move. Posted at the Washington Metro field office, she suddenly found herself with a nine-to-five workday, and time to spare for a relationship. She cautioned agents on the perils of substance abuse and post-traumatic stress, dismally unable to counsel herself. By the time she met Shane Isaacs, boredom had curdled to anger.

"Six years hostage rescue, six years employee assistance." Shane closed the file and contemplated

June. "You're settled in D.C. Why do you want this transfer?"

Stork-like legs carried him across his office. He was gangly and looked like he might not bend in the right places. He defied her doubt and folded himself behind his desk. Myopic eyes, full of intelligence, gazed at her intently. Thick lenses perched exactly halfway up his nose. He reminded her of a college professor, the sort to offer encouragement right up until the final exam. You only found out later that you'd flunked.

Watching his eyes blink, she heard herself say, "I'm bored to tears in employee assistance."

"Are you always so honest?"

"Yes, sir."

Except for the blinking, his gaze didn't waver. "After the hostage incident, you told debriefing you didn't think you could do it again."

"Right." He hadn't consulted her file. She knew her statement wasn't in the report.

"So you're afraid and you're bored. Anything else?"

"Lately I've been aware of some anger, sir."

He laughed. "That's useful." The look he gave her was serious, assessing. "Do you still carry the Browning?"

"Yes, sir."

"You'll be working violent crimes cases, bank robbery and kidnapping. And we have room for a negotiator. I don't need a sharpshooter, but I can use your social work skills. Interested?"

"Yes, sir."

* * * * *

"You fucking over-achiever," Charlene had accused.

"I'm moving to Boston."

"I don't want you in the field. It's dangerous. And I have no intention of moving to Boston."

"I didn't ask you to come."

"Just like that? This isn't something you want to talk over with your lover of six years?"

"I'm not your only partner. You don't deserve a conversation."

"Hey. I never bought tickets to pairs skating."

"I thought monogamy came with the mortgage. My mistake."

Charlene reached for her. "Come on, baby. If that's the way you want it. Let's talk." It was a familiar tone, but it no longer sounded sexy.

"I've been talking for six years." She shrugged off the hand. "I want to get back to the field."

"Who is she? Some babe in Boston?"

"I'm not leaving you for a woman, Charlene. I'm just going back to work."

Her desk was in the violent crimes section. Down the hall, a pin-up photo gallery decorated the fugitive squad's workspace. White collar crimes rounded out the seventh floor, with the supervisors' offices at each end. Boston's SAC, the special agent in charge, and the assistant SACs, enjoyed the executive suites on floor six. Two floors down was administrative support; a level below that contained a library of case files and a room devoted entirely to internal building security.

A stack of brown-tipped files, indicating bank

robbery cases, covered her desk. Every other inch of the shared pre-fab cubicle was being used by Al Rahman.

"Don't touch anything," he said.

"May I sit down?" Al's case files were stacked on her chair.

"No time. Shane wants to see you."

Like June, Al was new to the violent crimes squad, but he'd quickly usurped the space. In his mid-fifties, with a wiry build and handsome salt-and-pepper hair, he'd joined the Bureau as a C.P.A. Because he spoke fluent Arabic, he'd done most of his twenty-four years at headquarters, in counter-intelligence. Several of those had been spent under-cover. He hadn't offered the details, and June hadn't asked. She opened a folder and glanced through typed witness statements.

He said, "Don't get those out of order."

She pushed the folder aside and leaned a hip on her desk. His thermos sat on top of her in-basket. An Egyptian-American, Al lunched in Chinatown and drank Vietnamese drip coffee, thicker and more bitter than Italian espresso. She wondered if Al, like herself, spent less time sleeping than he'd like to.

His pencil traveled quickly down a list of teller numbers, entering dates next to the encoded information. He smiled. "Absenteeism pattern. Think I'll have a talk with Teller Watkins."

The Bureau was trying to retrain agents like Al to use less paper and more computer time. Except for the techies in Science, and the intelligence research specialists, most agents preferred to keep hard copies. Like the miser and his gold, or the gambler with a

16

lucky deck of cards, special agents liked the goods in hand.

Al's pencil started on another list. "Did you talk that guy down?"

"Yeah."

"How long?"

"Fifty-seven minutes."

He nodded. "Go see Shane." His cheekbones bracketed a hawkish nose. Thin lips betrayed no emotion. Dark lashes hid his eyes as he bent over his paperwork. "See you later, sure-shot."

Shane was stooped in the door of his office. He topped her by four inches but his habit of slouching brought them closer to eye level. June's broad shoulders, Charlene had once told her, made her look taller. Shane's strawberry-blond hair was thinning on top. The receding line made his forehead longer. He had a habit of staring, then blinking, snake-like, while he absorbed information.

He closed the file he'd been reading and pushed it into her hands. "Conference room, five minutes." He paused to gulp coffee. "Coffee?" he asked automatically.

"No, thanks." He craned his neck, continuing to read upside down while she turned pages. The powdery residue of artificial sweetener clung to the edge of his cup. It made her want to sneeze. "Do you mind?"

He straightened a fraction. "Four minutes." He glided down the hall.

Shane's mind measured the world in microseconds. From his point of view, four minutes held volumes of information. His personnel file was a lesson in gruesome fact-finding. He'd been a member of the FBI Disaster Squad, processing finger, palm and footprints to identify crime victims, and bodies from plane crashes. Before that, he'd been an evidence-response technician for a New York bomb squad. He sorted information in fractional increments, as if he had a stop-motion camera behind his eyes instead of normal optic nerves.

She read the file standing in his doorway. It wasn't worth the effort to fight Al for a place to sit. She'd already absorbed most of the report — a 32-year-old rape victim, two months ago, in March. The rapist had been shot and killed, and local press had dubbed it the Good Sam shooting. The victim had been severely beaten. No suspects had been found. June flipped to the back of the file. Police photos, taken at the hospital, showed a broken nose, hollows under the eyes already discolored. She stared at the bruised face of Amelia Wright, then closed the file and headed for the elevator.

The formal conference room was on the sixth floor. The table was real, not the push-together surfaces used by the agents upstairs. Framed pictures hung on the walls; the chairs had high backs. At the moment, only two seats were occupied, one by Shane, a second by a paunchy man she didn't know. He had the kind of overweight build that looked powerful in a business suit but fell apart in vacation clothes. Square palms rested on a leather briefcase. She noted his wedding band; the companion finger on his right hand bore a jeweled ring. The expensive briefcase snapped open. He sorted through files, selected one and set it aside.

"Agent Gavin," Shane said, "I'd like you to meet the Bureau's assistant director for the criminal investigative division, Edward Colt. In the field, he's special agent in charge."

Colt extended a hand. An executive from head-quarters carried political tendrils like most agents trailed paperwork. She returned the handshake. His ring seemed gaudy, the stone set in a crest-engraved band. It looked like the kind of ring that high school seniors flashed at the prom.

"Agent Gavin." His voice was heavy. "Your father fought the Nazis, didn't he? I mean, he flew missions against the Arabs that were helping the Nazis."

She cleared her throat. "Yes, sir."

"A night flyer. He had excellent eyesight, I understand. The same as you."

Her lips tightened. "He piloted bombers, and he also flew retrieval missions to recover downed pilots. I've never flown planes, sir."

She remembered, as a child, holding a newspaper across the room and teasing him until he read the small print. Then he took the paper and held it for her. His vocabulary was bigger; otherwise she matched him word for word. At the range, his old service revolver was too heavy for her eight-year-old hands, so he'd bought her the Olympic. By the time she was ten, she was placing five-shot groups in the target's center X at fifty meters. She could still hear her mother's protests as they left the chores unfinished on Saturday, loading .45 caliber ammunition for her father's Colt Gold Cup.

"You want your little girl to grow up like a boy?

19

She's got no manners and no sense for anything but guns. You're off to a good start, if that's what you want."

Her father had laughed. "Got your daddy's eyes, don't you, honey?"

She stared at a point over Colt's shoulder.

He said, "I wish I could use those pretty eyes of yours now, Gavin, but there's no need for a specialist." He tapped the file and passed it to Shane. "Maybe you'll like this one. Two months ago, Amelia Wright walked out of a nightclub. She was pulled into an alley and raped, then someone shot her attacker. She got herself beat up pretty good. The rapist got killed. She identified the shooter as male, no other descriptive details. And no witnesses. The nine-one-one call came from the bar." He stared at June. "It's a queer joint."

She crossed her arms, forcing herself to concentrate.

"We want the gunman," he said. "This so-called Good Sam shooter is no innocent bystander. We're already investigating a series of kidnappings in Maryland and Virginia. Bank officers are abducted, and after minimal negotiation, a ransom is paid. The banks are keeping quiet. From a kidnapper's point of view, it's low-stress work." He paused. "About two years ago, after the payoff, some of the banks were hit for the exact same amount of the ransom."

Shane blinked. "The bank pays the ransom, and then someone robs them again for the same amount?"

"That's the procedure. First a kidnapping, then a robbery. The amounts are always the same."

June asked, "What's the connection to Wright?

There was no robbery, and there's been no kidnapping that we're aware of."

"Wright was raped in the alley behind Boston Consumer's Mutual. On that night, Good Sam gained access to the bank and made an electronic transfer of funds. That's how all the robberies are done — by getting into the operating system and creating user IDs. And last night, as he was leaving his health club, a bank vice president was abducted. The ransom demand was made within an hour. It matches the amount of the stolen funds."

"The robbery was two months ago," Shane said. "How can you steal a ransom before there's been a kidnapping?"

"It's backwards, but it's the same bank, and the amounts match exactly. It's also the most expensive action to date. Three point one million."

June shook her head. "Whoever's stealing from the banks can't hurt the kidnappers. It doesn't connect."

"Kidnappers panic at anything that draws attention. Consumer's Mutual isn't keeping a low profile like the others. In fact, they're damn near hysterical."

June asked, "What makes you think the Good Sam shooter was in the bank? Maybe he was on his way to rob the automatic teller. Or just an avenging citizen."

"The computer logged the exact time of the illegal transfer. The nine-one-one call was made within minutes. Good Sam was in the alley with Wright because he robbed the bank."

Shane said, "My unit isn't working that robbery case."

Colt looked angry, almost menacing, June thought. The amount of emotion he showed surprised her. She wondered what it was about this case that was getting to him.

He said, "I'm coordinating a task force at headquarters. We took this one because of the way the computer systems files were used. It matches the other robberies that we're investigating."

June could tell it galled Shane that an important case on his turf had been usurped.

He asked, "How was the bank's security breached?"

Colt said, "All of the alarm systems were off-line. The cameras were off and the alley door was open. It leads to the offices, not the vaults. But that's all he needed. He got into the computer operating files from an inside terminal. This guy wants it to be absolutely clear that he's in town."

"Bank personnel?"

"A manager suddenly relocated. We got a tip that he's in Mexico."

"So the robber bribed the inside help. That means he's been around before, probably in the bank."

"There's no security film from the night of the robbery, and Wright couldn't provide a detailed description. We need more information about Good Sam."

"You seem certain that he's still in the area," June said.

"I think he's been waiting for the kidnappers."

Shane asked, "Have there been any breaks with the other kidnapping cases?"

Colt scowled. "I've got agents investigating in each state. No one was hurt and the banks aren't cooperating. They don't like the press. But this one's different. Good Sam knew the kidnappers would hit Boston. I want this guy."

"The trail is two months old," June pointed out.

Colt twisted his ring until the jewel pressed his palm. "We've been doing surveillance on the girl."

"With what cause?"

Shane shot her a warning look.

"There was a chance he'd go after Wright, if he thought she saw him. She's the only one we know of, besides the dead rapist, who's even been close to Good Sam."

Shane asked, "Are you continuing surveillance?"

"If she were a risk, he'd have done something by now. If he thought she saw him, he'd have shot her too, not just her rapist. It's not about Wright anymore. We've got a kidnap victim to recover. If she can tell us something about Good Sam, now's the time. Her trauma's worn off, so question her again. Pick the scabs. See what she remembers."

"You'll need a negotiator," Shane suggested, "to secure the bank officer's release."

"My team's already on it. The kidnapping is top priority." Colt turned to June. "You're on Wright. I like to use a woman for this sort of thing. It's more sympathetic." The briefcase clicked shut. "Don't waste time. I want daily updates." He didn't bother with handshakes on his way out.

"Welcome to the baby-sitting task force." Shane handed her the file left by Colt. "Surveillance data. Colleagues, best friends and private conversations."

Chapter 3

"Forward paddle!"

The cry came from behind her. Amelia's thighs gripped the raft and she wedged her left heel into the bottom of the rubber boat. The six-person raft lurched into white water.

The rafting guide yelled, "Forward!"

All six paddlers responded. Shoulders straining, Amelia reached for the water. The nose of the raft bucked and slammed down. Anchored by her legs, she plunged her paddle into the river.

"Right turn!"

Again, her paddle moved water, backstroking once, twice, three times. The raft altered course, swinging in the current. She saw the boulder inches from the stern, its menacing bulk no longer a threat. Caught in the rapids, they slipped past. In front of her, the black pony tail of BJ Honda danced on his shoulders. He tucked his paddle between the boat and his muscular calf. His camera, secured to his chest by a thick strap, pointed downriver.

"Back paddle!"

They obeyed, and the raft slowed imperceptibly. BJ, using high-speed film, recorded the cascade.

"Hang on," the voice behind her warned.

Amelia lifted her paddle and braced. The river threw itself free of the bank, and the raft followed, plunging over the falls. As the water returned to earth, they rushed to meet it. BJ's ponytail flew out behind him. Over his shoulder, she followed the angle of his lens, straight down. Then they were swallowed, engulfed in a torrent of noise and churning motion. She smiled. As usual, BJ got it all on film.

Water spewed and she was flung back. The bow searched for the current, found it and surged forward. She paddled with all her strength, fighting to keep pace with the river's descent.

Amelia upended a black waterproof bag, hastily dumping the contents. In the back of her Jeep, camping gear and wet clothes spilled out, accompanied by the stench of mildew. She yanked the cord on a supply pouch, scattering crumpled food wrappers. A candy bar, still unopened, landed in the pile. She grabbed it, tearing cellophane with her teeth. Slumped against the bumper, she chewed intently on peanuts and chocolate. BJ, already tidy in dry clothes, was carefully repacking his camera bags. He stowed them neatly around her laundry.

"Bite?" Still chewing caramel, she offered him the candy.

"No, thank you."

She'd never known him to eat sugar. Between photo assignments, he practiced yoga and grew his own organic food. He focused his camera to capture adventure, instinctively snapping the pictures she put into words. Aside from his appallingly healthy habits, she liked BJ.

She wasn't surprised that Marj, their editor at *Outdoors Woman* magazine, had paired them for this trip. Marj commanded her work with a mix of business savvy and sensitivity. BJ was gregarious where Amelia had grown shy. He possessed stores of patience and extended them to her, insulating her when her nerves felt like spliced wire. And they were both gay, which made the camping bearable.

She finished her candy bar. "Can we stop for dinner?"

He wrinkled his nose. "We're in the Maine wilderness. I doubt there's a decent vegetarian meal for miles."

"Come on. I'm wet and cold and starving. Be a butch and buy me a steak."

"Don't even joke about it." He shuddered.

"I never joke about starvation."

He rummaged in the Jeep, producing one of his tie-dyed sweatshirts and a pair of her wrinkled khakis. "Get some dry clothes on, love. We'll stop for Chinese in Portland."

"I can't eat Chinese," she mumbled.

She abandoned her protest and stripped quickly. After days on the river, modesty was of no consequence. Spring rafting was frigid; once the wetsuits came off, it was a race to stay warm. By the time her article appeared on newsstands, vacationers would be packing for days of milder rapids and summer heat. But her words would describe the thrill of riding snowmelt — high, fast and dangerous.

She tugged his sweatshirt over her head. "Great trip, even though you wimped out on your share of the paddling."

He flexed his biceps. "Art is more important than action."

She pushed him off the bumper and tossed him the car keys. "If I have to eat vegetables, you have to drive."

June opened her eyes as a car motor idled then died. She sat up slightly. Across the street, headlights extinguished. Her dash clock showed almost ten. Twilight had faded hours ago. In another month, the long spring dusk would lighten to summer evening.

Recently, Amelia had moved out of Boston. The beach cottage, north of the city in Newburyport, belonged to her editor. The corner lot gave the little bungalow precious extra square feet.

The street dead-ended at grass-covered dunes. From her parking space, June could see a thread of dark ocean. Waves marched on the beach. Their melancholy roll call reached her through the open window. She used her own car, rather than one of the Bureau's customized, electronics-laden sedans. The Porsche had been a protest purchase after the break-up. Saving money for six years had been a bore.

Waiting as the salt-crusted air grew chill, she'd resisted the urge to go speeding up the empty drag. Not that there was anywhere to race to — the clam huts and ice cream stands were closed. Tired of the ocean's disquiet, she'd slotted a tape into the dash. Before she left Portsmouth, Bass had tossed a cassette into her car.

"I got that when Brenda moved out. Give it a try."

She swore under her breath. She should have known he'd be checking up on her. She thought she'd been discreet.

He said, "Come for a visit. Beer and fried clams. My treat."

Bass was smarter than he let on, and he had eclectic taste in music. By the time Amelia drove up, Elvis Costello was singing "I'm Not Angry."

Under a streetlight, the Jeep looked splotchy. June could make out bright red patches under streaks of mud. Amelia opened the back and gathered up an armload of laundry. June turned off the music and walked toward the light.

When she was easily visible, she stopped. "Ms. Wright. My name is June Gavin. I'm a federal agent." She held up her credentials. "Marj MacMichael told me you'd be back this evening."

Amelia glanced at the Porsche. Ignoring June, she trotted through the gate to the cottage. June followed, surprised by Amelia's nonchalance. On the porch, she anchored a camping pack over her shoulder and unlocked the door. There was a thud as the pack dropped inside. She disappeared after it.

The porch light came on. "ID."

June held her wallet under the light, then snatched her hand back as the door slammed shut. At the same time, she stuck her shoe over the threshold, wincing as pressure-treated wood crimped the leather.

"Get your foot out of my door and tell my editor I quit." The door swung open in preparation for another foot-bruising slam.

June braced her arm across the jamb. "Don't put yourself out of a good job, Ms. Wright. I didn't give your editor much choice."

"My editor doesn't get intimidated." The door crashed into June.

She added body weight to support her arm. Exasperated, she said, "Amelia, will you please stop hitting me?" The door halted, briefly and mercifully motionless. Half inside, she could see a hardwood floor. Wet clothes stank of mildew. "I just want to talk to you."

"I spent all day splashing around in ice water. Then I drove home with a man who thinks dinner is stir-fried green beans. Go away." The door began to swing.

"Are you hungry?"

"So what?"

"There's a place up the highway that serves until eleven." The door no longer seemed an imminent threat. "Why don't you let me treat you to a decent meal?"

"Go away." The door didn't move. Strength was seeping out of her objections.

"You know I won't. Tonight, maybe. But I'll come back tomorrow. Don't prolong it, Amelia. I'll buy you dinner tonight."

Amelia kicked the pack out of the way and stepped outside. "How'd you get my editor to tell you my schedule?"

"She wanted to know what kind of car I drive."

Amelia smiled at the private joke. "That sounds like Marj. Is that your Porsche?"

"Yes."

"The men that came around before drove Buicks."

"I'm sorry." She knew she was apologizing for more than her colleagues' taste in sedans.

In the porchlight, the hollows under Amelia's eyes were stained, not with bruises but fatigue. An irregular bump marred the line of her nose, the telltale sign of a break. Other evidence of physical battering had faded, but gauntness etched her face, stretching the skin beneath messy curls. Under a baggy sweatshirt, Amelia Wright looked scrawny. Only the sore spots on June's arm warned that she'd lost weight, not strength.

She resisted the urge to rub her elbow. "Let's get dinner."

"What did you say your name was?" Amelia followed the broad-shouldered agent back to the street.

"June Gavin. Please call me June."

"Don't you want me to call you Special Agent or something?"

"That's not necessary." She unlocked the Porsche.

It wasn't black, as Amelia had first thought, but a dark, sedate blue. June, tall and crisp in a suit jacket and slacks, walked around to the driver's side. Her blond hair fell in a sleek, blunt cut. Healthy and fit, she looked like she'd stepped out of a weekend catalogue. Predictable colors — beige and blue. Dull, Amelia assessed. But the Porsche had potential.

She climbed in. "I thought G-men drove Buicks."

"Good thing I'm not a G-man."

"You're a government agent, aren't you?"

"I'm a federal agent. No one calls us G-men anymore, not even the press." A hint of a smile crossed her lips. "Buicks are a little boring, don't you think?" The Porsche pulled smoothly away from the curb.

Fatigued and restless, Amelia fidgeted. The bucket seats were cream leather; dials and indicator lights gleamed. There was a car phone, but she detected nothing sinister, no secret radios, no gun rack. She couldn't see a gun at all.

June glanced at her. "What are you looking for?"

"Your gun."

"I'm wearing a shoulder holster."

"Oh." She looked out the windshield. "The Buick agents — they were assholes."

"I can imagine."

"No you can't. You have no idea."

"Tell me." It wasn't a challenge. She made it sound like a suggestion, like what to order for dinner.

"I don't want to talk about it."

They turned from the coastal route onto the

interstate and the car picked up speed. Still restless, Amelia fiddled with the stereo. An Elvis Costello tape popped into her hand.

"I just got that," June said. "Do you listen to him?"

"No." She dropped it on the dash. "I guess you get paid pretty well. I mean, to be driving a Porsche."

June laughed. "Do you like it? This is a nineteen eighty-eight nine-thirty Turbo. Used, but only one owner. I just got divorced and I didn't want another mortgage. The car represents my half of the house."

Amelia sat silently. She'd thought, she'd been sure, June was a lesbian. She said bluntly, "I thought you were gay."

"I am. I was with a woman for six years."

Amelia stared at her. "What happened?"

"I asked for a transfer. Charlene, the woman I was with, still lives in D.C. She was sleeping around." June shrugged. "I would have left anyway. I was too . . . stationary."

Amelia mulled the information, thinking of Bryanna. Sweet Bryanna, still in Boston, who couldn't accept that the relationship was over. She asked, "Do you miss her?"

"No. Do you miss Bryanna?"

She gripped the seat. Her hands slipped on the clammy leather. "What the hell do you know about Bryanna?"

June asked patiently, "Did the men in the Buicks talk to you about the rape?"

Amelia's stomach clenched. She groped for the window controls. June lowered it from her side.

"They probably asked you a lot of questions and

32

then acted like you were lying. I'll bet they accused you of not cooperating and threatened to expose your deceit. Is that about right?"

Amelia kept her lips clamped. The taste of nausea coated her tongue. The car turned from the interstate into a tourist-trap parking lot. A neon sign was making a fuss about steak, lobster and Micholob.

June faced her. "Some agents still work that way. Most don't, not anymore. Try to understand, Amelia, this case isn't about you. The people in charge want the man who shot your rapist. They're frustrated, and they took it out on you. I'm sorry. It's a lousy way to get treated."

"They said they were watching." The words fought their way through clenched teeth. "One of those . . . bastards . . . said I'd never be safe."

She closed her eyes but the memory throbbed. Her throat ached and her cheeks felt hot, like a fever. She saw his face — twisted, flaccid lips. The picture warped and his mouth came closer — moist, a rim of sweat, spit. Like a backed-up drain, the urge to scream filled her chest; his glove blocked the sound. She couldn't breathe.

Dimly, she was aware of movement. Her window was all the way down.

"Take a breath," a voice repeated. "Take a breath."

Slowly, her lungs responded. Then she was gasping. Frantically, she wiped her face but she wasn't crying.

June began to talk. It took a while for the words to make sense. ". . . court order to get a wire tap . . . probable cause . . . thought the shooter might try to contact you." Her voice was calm. The sound grew stronger. "They probably argued that it was for your own protection. I'm sorry, Amelia. Does any of this really surprise you?"

Air had returned. "No," she whispered. Whatever she felt, she wasn't surprised.

"Good." June nodded. "I know all the details. You, Bryanna, your boss. We're going to talk about it one more time." Her tone was crisp. "There's been a kidnapping, Amelia. A bank vice president. You'll hear about it in tomorrow's news. We think the Good Sam shooter robbed the bank, and we think he can help us find the kidnappers. We're hoping you can help us find Good Sam. Questioning you is routine follow-up. That's all there is to it."

Her no-nonsense voice matched her clothes. Plain and practical. Amelia listened to the reassuring tone, and the feeling of nausea faded.

June smiled. "Are you still hungry?" The dash clock showed ten-forty.

Amelia cleared her throat. "I want to see my file."

June's mouth pulled, like she'd stubbed her toe and bit back the pain. "The file's a bitch. It's full of a lot of stuff that doesn't matter. And your hospital records. Leave it alone, okay?"

She had a wide forehead, like her shoulders, and brown eyes. Amelia would have guessed blue, to match blond hair. The blond-brown combination was unusual. The dark eyes reminded Amelia of antique furniture — a visible glow under a lot of wear and tear. Her nose was too long, lips full over a strong chin.

"Come on," June said, "let's eat."

* * * * *

The beefy twang of country and western drifted
over a cluster of pick-ups at the roadside lounge. The
restaurant had already emptied in favor of the music
and booze next door. June led the way to a booth,
standard burgundy steakhouse decor. A waitress
followed them to a table.

"Good evening, ladies. The kitchen closes in
fifteen minutes. Can I put your order in now?"

Amelia stared blankly at a menu.

June asked, "Steak or lobster?"

"Steak." She spoke tonelessly.

"One steak dinner," June ordered. "Potato, salad,
the works. I'll have a side salad, please, and water."
She closed her menu.

"Any cocktails tonight?"

Amelia said, "No. Just water."

"How do you like your steak?"

"Rare."

June tried not to grimace at the thought of rare
meat. The waitress brought water and returned to
the kitchen.

Amelia was rubbing her temples. "I hate it that
you know things about me."

"An investigation often feels like an invasion of
privacy."

"What about you," her low tone accused. "I didn't
think the Feds went for queers."

"The government hired me because I have a
talent for shooting straight."

Amelia pounced. "Did you ever kill anyone?"

"Yes."

She looked more alert across the table. "Why?"

June sipped ice water. "The man I shot was threatening to blow up a plane full of hostages."

"What did he say?"

"I wasn't negotiating, just watching."

Watching his head, through her sights, and concentrating on the way his scratchy-looking beard had filled the gap between sights and target.

"What do you see when you look at the target?" Her father had always asked the same question.

"I look at the target, then the sights."

One time, though, he asked, "What do you see right before you look at the sights and pull the trigger?"

She grinned, knowing the answer. "I look at the gaps between the sights and the target." She explained his instructions back to him. "To make sure they're even."

"How big is the gap?"

She held herself very still, the target pistol steady in her twelve-year-old's grip. "It's big," she said slowly. She frowned, doubting her answer. "Right before I pull the trigger, it's all I see." She turned to him, expecting correction.

His thoughtful frown matched hers. "That's right," he said. "That's just how I would say it." He had gripped her shoulder. "If you don't see the gap, don't pull the trigger. But when the gap is all you see, you're dead on."

The investigators had tormented her, questioned her without pause or mercy. Why had she failed to use the long-range rifle? Why had she taken the shot with her handgun? She hadn't told them about the gap, but she'd seen it more clearly than she'd ever seen anything. When her bullet broke the bridge of his nose, the gap had filled with fire. Flames haloed his head. He'd fallen before she realized the plane wasn't on fire. Eventually, the investigators stopped screaming, and the special agent in charge placed a commendation in her file.

Had her father been alive, she might have told him. It was his nightmare, after all. He'd never talked about the war, but she saw planes exploding, flames crawling skyward. She'd asked him, once, why he'd joined the forest service.

"Some people run from their nightmares. Some people walk right into them."

She couldn't remember when her dreams began. Not when he was alive. In high school, probably, after he died. In college, she'd worked extra waitress shifts to pay for a single room. Roommates had laughed when she fell out of bed, but the late-night comedy got stale.

"Sleep walking."

She made the same excuse every morning because there was no way to explain a tidal wave of flame so hot that even the air burned. She tried to run, and fell, legs pinned. She didn't know who he'd seen trapped in the heat of a wrecked plane, its exploded engine gunning black fumes. She didn't recognize the boy with tears on his face, fingers seared from hot metal, mouth screaming, his legs burning first, then his body. She saw him through her father's eyes and knew that for him it wasn't nightmare but memory. He ran into the flames and she tried to follow, tried to run, and fell. And woke up.

She made it through college by studying late and

37

working breakfast shifts. At the diner, she met the local cops, poured their coffee and buttered their toast. She knew who liked jelly doughnuts or plain, and whether they loaded their revolvers with .38 Special or .357 magnum cartridges. The local gun club had been easy to find.

"Where'd you learn to shoot?" they asked.

"My father taught me."

Away from her mother's disapproving glare, she'd practiced every day and won every weekend competition. At night, fighter planes exploded in her dreams and sent her spinning to the floor like twisted metal.

Water splashed on the table as the waitress re-filled their glasses. Plates of food had arrived.

Amelia was stabbing her potato. "So you shot the big bad terrorist. Then what happened?"

"The hostages lived and he died. Case closed." She ate a forkful of salad.

Amelia was silent, slicing red meat. "How do you keep your strength up eating lettuce?"

"I eat cheese and eggs. No meat."

Her knife traced the grill lines on her steak. "Does it offend you that I do?"

"You don't offend me."

She abandoned the knife and fork without taking a bite. "I used to love steak. The thought of it still appeals to me, but I . . . can't eat. BJ's vegetarian."

"The photographer?"

"You should know."

"Tell me about your trip."

Amelia became animated as she talked. June

leaned into the table, drawn by her enthusiasm. "Spring rafting is fantastic. The river's high, really fast." Her eyes gleamed. "We went over a waterfall. The force of it pushes you under then spits you out. You can't fight it. The river overpowers everything." She sat back. As quickly as it had peaked, her energy abated. "Do you like sports?" It was a polite question.

"I started running and weight-training in college. The only sport I've ever been competitive in is shooting."

The sergeant from the local force had bought a new nine-millimeter Beretta, and he badgered her all the way to the practice range. He fired nine rounds and reloaded.

"You gotta admit, that's a beautiful gun." He caressed the blue-finished barrel. "Here you go. See what it's all about."

The Beretta had a shorter barrel than her Olympic, and fixed sights. She studied his target. His grouping was good, a little off-center left.

"Where do you want 'em, Sarge?"

He laughed. "Brassy recruit. Just hit the X, little girl. That'll do fine." Nine shots obliterated the bull's-eye. "Atta way, baby," he crowed. "Hey, there's a competition this weekend. You and me, girl. We'll go together."

It was a muddy day. The sergeant gripped his gun too tightly, spreading his group. A man she didn't know stepped up to the mark and extended one hand. He held the oddest-looking gun she'd ever seen, and fired a club-record score. She approached him after he'd claimed his medal.

"Ah, the young lady with the perfectly aimed High Standard." His British accent enthralled her.

"Excuse me. I've never seen a handgun like that."

He smiled from beneath a tidy mustache. "My dear, this is a Hammerli match pistol. It fires a twenty-two caliber long rifle round and has a five-lever set-trigger adjustable to within fractions of an ounce." She smoothed a finger over the wood grips. "Walnut," he said. "Fitted to my hand, of course."

There was a pressure on her shoulder. It was the sergeant, pulling her away.

"Accuracy," the accented voice called. "Never sacrifice it."

She climbed into the sergeant's pick-up. Tires bit gravel.

"Don't be impressed," he growled. "Apple pie manners, but that's a sweet potato faggot."

He pulled a flask of bourbon from the glove box. It began to rain. A mile from campus, he rolled the truck into a ditch. She got out to help him push and found herself pinned against the fender, his foul-smelling breath in her ear, his erection nudging her thighs. He groped her crotch.

She elbowed his gut. "Get off me, Sarge. You're a sore loser and a mean drunk." She managed to turn. "I said, get off!"

He crushed her breast. His belt buckle was undone, hands fumbling with his fly.

For a dizzying moment, the hands she saw weren't puffy and freckled; they were smooth and lean, like her father's. And the voice wasn't the sergeant's scruffy drawl.

She heard soft tones. "Come here, honey."

Her feet slipped and she half-fell. The sergeant had exposed himself. He stood like a bull let loose from a pen, head swinging, summoning courage to charge. Her fist made a tight, fast arc, and her two front knuckles connected with his chin. He landed on his butt, penis drooping sadly. She made it to the front bumper before she started throwing up. Then she hiked back to campus.

In the dorm, she took a shower and taped her knuckles. She tried to sleep, shuddering awake each time she felt a hand, or something else, between her legs. She rolled out of bed and stood in the shower until someone banged on the bathroom door and complained. At dawn, she was early for the breakfast shift. The sergeant didn't show.

She missed the next two competitions. Alone in her room, she had taped a target to the wall, sitting in bed and dry-firing until her hand cramped. Back at the pistol range, the sickening feeling of her father's touch faded. In her sleep, the fire-drenched nightmares flared.

Amelia had picked up her fork and was prodding a tomato.

The waitress came back. "I guess you're not big eaters tonight. Can I wrap that for you?"

"No." Amelia pushed her plate away. "Thanks anyway." June took out a credit card. Amelia said, "I should try some of BJ's health food. He gets so pissed when I order meat." She half-smiled. "It's kind of fun to watch."

June signed the bill. She asked, more out of habit than interest, "Why do you want to make him angry?"

"Anyone but me."

June drove back along the coastal route as Amelia dozed. She idled the Porsche and touched her shoulder.

Amelia snapped awake. "Why do I feel like I'm getting home too late from a bad date?"

"In that case, maybe I should take a spin around the block and wake up the neighbors."

Amelia almost laughed. "Yeah, well, see you around."

"I'll be over tomorrow."

"What?"

"It's Saturday. I'll bring lunch."

"I won't cooperate. I only went out with you because I like your car."

June revved the engine. "I'm delighted. I always hoped I'd be more popular with a Porsche."

"If you want to win a popularity contest, change your wardrobe."

"Excuse me?"

"Add some color." Amelia got out of the car but ducked her head back in. "All this navy blue, June. It's a little boring."

June waited until Amelia was safely in the cottage, then she slammed a cassette in the tape deck and stomped the accelerator. She left loud skidmarks on the curb.

Chapter 4

A breeze stirred the curtain and moonlight washed the glass. By the window, a seated figure cast a still shadow. June moved silently into her apartment. She slipped into the kitchen and turned on the stove light. An empty plate was on the counter. A note on the refrigerator, scrawled in shaky cursive, said *Lasagna*. She ignored the refrigerator. Opening the freezer, she removed an icy bottle. Two glasses waited by the plate. She carried glasses and bottle into the living room.

From the armchair, a formal voice said, "Good evening, June."

The low contralto quickened her pulse and soothed her nerves. Gretchen Jensen had the loveliest voice she'd ever heard.

"Hi, Gretch." She adjusted the switch on a table lamp and the soft light stole some of the shadows.

"Ah. You look tired." Gretchen made the ordinary words sound like music.

June settled into a matching chair. She poured the vodka and handed Gretchen a drink. When she'd first come to look at the apartment, there'd only been one armchair by the window.

"She had it converted a year ago," the realtor had said. "When her . . . companion passed on. It hasn't been rented yet. I don't think she knows which she wants less, the rental income or the empty space. She lives downstairs, of course." She fussed with a set of keys and led the way up narrow stairs. "This beautiful old neighborhood is called Beacon Hill. Miss Jensen was famous once — someone at the office told me she sang opera. On the radio. Can you imagine?"

June stepped inside and stared at maple floors, Oriental rugs and arched windows. A lonely armchair sat before the curtained view. In it was a wrinkled woman wearing floral silk, her silver hair in a majestic coiffure.

"Miss Jensen." The realtor frowned. "We agreed you'd have the furniture moved last week."

"Yes, yes. Those young men you sent carried everything down. A lifetime's treasures, packed and ready for a white elephant sale. Not even a complete collection. Hello, dear." The lovely voice caressed her, as intimate as a kiss. "Have you come to live in my home?"

June brushed aside the realtor's flurried apology. The worn rugs muted her footsteps. At the window, she swept back the curtain. Stately homes sat on a tree-lined street. She glimpsed vine-covered courtyards and curlicue walks, as twisted as the wrought iron furniture nestled inside.

"My friend and I enjoyed this view for years." Gretchen whispered the words, a lyrical confidence.

June said, "Then there must be a matching chair."

The wrinkled face brightened. "You are so right."

"I don't have much furniture. I left most of it with someone else in Washington, D.C."

"A lovely city." Pale eyes studied her. "Unless you're too caught up in memories to look at the scenery. When the weather's bad, I watch C-Span. Keep current, dear."

June let the curtain fall. "If I live here, may I borrow the other chair?"

"They're a set. It makes no sense to keep them apart."

Behind them, the realtor began to drone about lease-signing and security deposits.

Gretchen waved her away. "We'll sort out that nonsense some other time. Put it in the mail, if you must." She had turned back to June. "Let's get clear on a few details. Do you like opera?"

One week later, June had carried the second armchair back upstairs. It didn't matter that she'd never cared for opera or overstuffed furniture. She'd already fallen in love with Gretchen Jensen.

Two weeks after moving in, she awoke from a nightmare to a noise in the apartment. Her weapon was in her hand before her bare feet touched the floor. In stoic calm, she flooded the living room with light and leveled the Browning at the chest of Gretchen's flannel bathrobe. Without a word, she returned to the bedroom, dropped the magazine and stowed the gun and ammunition in a locking case.

"For God's sake, Gretchen, I thought you were a prowler."

"I didn't mean to startle you, dear. I come upstairs when I can't sleep. I still have a key and I forget, really, that I'm not alone in the house anymore."

June sank into an armchair. When she could speak without strain, she said, "You're welcome anytime. I have to warn you, though, I'm often up half the night myself."

"Why don't you pour us a drink?" the sweet voice soothed.

Now, with the vodka cold on her tongue, she was tempted to tell Gretchen about the nightmares. But Gretchen's glass sat untouched on the side table, and the silver head had nodded back. June turned out the lamp. In gauzy moonlight, memories churned, coursing like a stream under the liquor's ice.

The vocation counselor, barely out of college

herself, had pushed a catalogue across the table. "You've done all your general requirements." She sounded proud. "That's really great. And there's still time to choose another major." She smiled sympathetically. "There aren't too many women in forestry."

June couldn't smile. The forest, where she'd always been at home, had betrayed her. The silent, beautiful woods had turned scratchy and loud. Instead of dappled leaves, she saw steaming workshirts, bulging forearms. Sweaty hands rubbed trees and stubbly throats yelled jokes, the camaraderie as stifling as a heat wave. Before Sarge, she hadn't noticed. Now every glance raked her skin until she thought she'd bleed; a gesture from a hundred yards stung like a slap.

The counselor's eyes were full of interest. "Any idea what you'd like to study?"

"What was your major?"

"Psychology. Then I got my master's in education. Learning new things is exciting, don't you think?"

June was thinking that she'd never noticed how a woman's breasts swelled when she laughed. She wanted to give a reason, to explain the woods. "I have allergies." It wasn't what she'd meant to say. "I want a major where I don't need antihistamines."

The counselor wore turquoise and silver rings, bangle bracelets and hoop earrings. She leaned over, flipping pages. "Here's a list of course descriptions." Her nails, like June's, were trimmed short. The catalogue bore the musky scent of her perfume.

"I have to think about it."

"Do you drink coffee?"

"Sure." She didn't. Every morning, she poured it

by the gallon into ceramic mugs. On break, she drank tea. Learning to drink coffee seemed suddenly important.

"Some of my friends hang out at a coffeehouse. A lot of them are psych majors." She scribbled an address. "They'd love to meet you, and you can ask some questions."

Later that night, seated at a crowded table, she listened to the women and forgot about the woods. She went home with the vocation counselor, trembling as they undressed each other, overwhelmed by soft, then urgent sensations. They fell on the bed. Palms caressed her, explored, embraced. Then fingers touched her breasts. She raised herself up, uncertain, but the counselor's hands were stroking again, a slow massage.

"Magnificent." She gripped June's shoulders. "You should lift weights. All this beautiful strength. You should train it, develop it." She smiled. "Mind and body."

Eagerly, June responded. She stopped trembling and touched gently, then with abandon. When she hesitated, the counselor guided her fingers and shuddered. June knelt. The counselor stroked her cheek, then softly pressed her down. June consumed her, first with her hands, then her mouth, sucking with passion-starved lips.

The counselor lay panting. "Forget the weights," she groaned. "You're perfect."

June covered her, pressing until she climaxed, then again until they were both shaking and soaking.

"Slow down, baby," the counselor gasped. "Oh God, slow down. We've got all night."

But June had wanted to spend every minute

loving the woman in her arms. Awake, and in love, she'd never have to sleep.

The next morning she parked behind Amelia's Jeep and climbed the steps to the porch. No one answered her knock. Holding a grocery bag, she peered through a picture window. Camping debris was everywhere. Aside from the cluttered equipment, the cottage looked empty. She turned to survey the beach. Low dunes formed a natural windbreak. A gusting breeze whipped the marsh grass, frothing the water. June left the groceries and hiked through the dunes.

The ocean lay between wide swaths of sand and horizon. She took sunglasses from her collar and shaded her eyes. Summer crowds were a month away. Scavenging gulls circled, then planted their feet; beach-walkers dug in, like slanted toothpicks. The sky, scuffed with clouds, was pale, as though a painter, after dabbing the waves, had run out of blue.

An isolated figure in a blaze orange jacket stood a hundred meters distant. Caught by the breeze, the jacket flared into purple and white lightning bolts. The pattern zapped across the shoulders and down each arm. The figure turned away. June advanced on the electric windbreaker.

Amelia turned her back, but not before she'd observed that June's professional clothes had given way to faded jeans and a pullover sweatshirt. A navy sweatshirt. She swung her arms, trying to unknot her shoulders.

"Tense?"

She whirled. June wore battered running shoes. Her hips and thighs bulged under soft denim. A purple polo shirt opened at her throat. Amelia eyed the color gratefully. Wind tugged the sweatshirt's hood. June looked bigger on the beach and, in backyard clothes, more normal.

Amelia faced the water. "There's not much surf here." She surprised herself by making conversation.

"I love the beach," June said. "I grew up in California, but I never lived on the coast."

"You're from Boston, aren't you?"

She chuckled. "When you live in rush hour traffic, it's easy to forget that Boston has a coastline."

Curiosity irritated her. "Where in California?"

"Wine country, in Napa Valley."

"I've heard it's beautiful."

"The grapes are gorgeous and the fires are devastating. My father worked for the forest service. He took me camping a lot, in the mountains." June took off her sunglasses. They hung on her chest.

She had full breasts, Amelia observed. Big and healthy, like the rest of her. "I know San Francisco and Santa Cruz, and I'll be going to San Diego soon."

"I asked your editor for a copy of your itinerary."

Amelia concentrated on the waves. "I think I hate you."

"You hate the intrusion. I don't blame you."

"I bet a lot of people hate you. Doesn't it get to you?"

"Why should it? You don't even know me."

Amelia rolled her shoulders. Rib muscles constricted. Pain was a second heartbeat, pulsing agony. She clamped her teeth. What she really wanted to do was scream, but she couldn't get a deep enough breath. Gradually, she became aware of a different pressure. Choked muscle began to loosen. The sensation sorted itself into strong fingers, kneading rhythmically, stripping soreness like a layer of dead skin.

She stepped away. "Don't touch me. If I want a massage, I'll pay a professional."

"You're right. I'm sorry. You looked like you were in pain." In the sunlight, June's eyes looked soft.

"I pulled a muscle on the rafting trip. It's an occupational hazard. Don't waste your time worrying."

June put on her sunglasses. "No problem. I left lunch on your porch. Do you want to eat?"

"What the hell is this? Do they teach you this crap in cop school?"

"I don't know what you're talking about. I never went to cop school."

"Excuse me. The FBI academy. This good cop, bad cop routine — just ditch it, okay?"

"For your information, that technique is hard to do solo."

"I don't put it past you." Amelia stalked up the beach, keeping a step ahead, aware that June could have caught her easily.

A mountain bike hung upside down, helmet and gloves hooked on the handlebars. Double-bladed paddles leaned in a corner; a kayak was secured in a rack. Canoes, June mused, must be too slow. Pink and purple, green and blue ropes snaked and coiled across the floor, surrounded by small mountains of boots and metal fasteners. An unrolled sleeping bag and unfolded laundry covered the couch. The furniture, blond wood and pastel fabric, faced the picture window.

June recalled that Amelia's editor owned the cottage. It was exactly what she would have expected in a city executive's summer home. But the camping gear clashed. She wondered if, without her editor's influence, Amelia would have pitched a tent. The dining area featured wood and glass, and an open bar. She unpacked a casserole and a loaf of bread.

"Who do you think you are, Mother Teresa on a mission to feed the poor?"

"I don't have a motherly bone in my body. And you're not poor. You've won at least one journalism award every year since you started writing for *Outdoors Woman*, and you're compensated handsomely."

Amelia's mouth compressed. "What else? Let's just get this over with."

June pushed aside laundry, making room on the couch. "You're thirty-two, which makes you six years younger than me. You studied journalism, I studied psych. Your favorite hobby is rock-climbing; at least, that's the one you do most often. You worked on the usual student rags in college, and your politics, on a map, are left of San Francisco, which is where you lived when you graduated Cal Berkeley. I attended the more sedate and conservative UC Davis campus. I thought I wanted to go into forestry, like my father."

"What changed your mind?"

"I slept with the college vocational counselor. By

morning, I'd changed my sexual orientation and my major."

Amelia hid a grin. "Go on."

"You won your first major writing award when you were twenty-six. *Outdoors Woman* baited you with freelance work for two years. Then Marj MacMichael took over as editor-in-chief. She got you on payroll and you relocated to Boston. The magazine's circulation went up the first year you were on regular staff."

"The FBI checked our subscription stats?"

"I looked that one up myself."

"What do you do with your spare time, when you're not invading people's privacy?"

"I've been winning shooting competitions since I was twelve. After college, I got my M.S.W. The Bureau recruited me after graduate school."

"Social work? How very touchy-feely."

"Not at first. I did hostage rescue for six years. Then I got sidetracked in employee assistance. Those were the touchy-feely years. Now I do bank robbery, kidnapping, and hostage negotiation."

"I'm beginning to feel like a hostage."

"Are you ready for lunch?"

Amelia moved cautiously toward the table. "What is all this?"

"Lasagna. I assume you have a microwave?"

"In the kitchen. You cooked lasagna?"

"Our housekeeper cooks for an army." She answered Amelia's questioning stare. "My landlady, who's eighty-two, shares her expensive vodka with me and doesn't charge nearly enough rent. So I hired a housekeeper."

"Sounds like domestic bliss."

June hefted the casserole. "I guess it is."

In the kitchen, she searched for serving utensils. A pattern of vines and fruit bordered plates and mugs. Not Amelia's dishes. She wondered if Amelia had cracked a cupboard. Curious, she opened the refrigerator and surveyed a jar of mustard, a carton of milk and a row of brown beer bottles.

"Now you're really getting personal." Amelia stood in the doorway, arms folded. The date on the milk had expired. June poured it down the drain. "So much for my morning cereal."

"Use beer. You've got plenty."

"I don't have any —" She yanked open the refrigerator. "Oh. That's ginseng beer, made by BJ, photographer, visual artist and vegetarian menace. He brews and bottles it himself." She held up a bottle. "It's non-alcoholic and tastes god-awful. I can't drink the real stuff. Alcohol makes me throw up."

The microwave beeped. June helped herself to a ginseng. "Do you want one?"

"No way. I'll drink water." At the table, Amelia watched her as she cut into the lasagna. She stared, horrified. "It's green."

June glanced up from her culinary surgery. "Spinach." Cheese had melted through the layers, alternating white and green. She passed Amelia a plate. "I thought you'd find it colorful."

"If you feed this to your landlady, it's no wonder she drinks."

June served herself and took a sip of ginseng. She winced. "Wow. That's strong."

"I warned you." Amelia watched as June began to eat. "I used to eat piles of pasta. Especially right before and after a climb. I couldn't get enough." She drew designs in the sauce. "After — it hurt to chew. And everything tasted like blood." She speared her noodles. They oozed cheese. "God, I swallowed so much blood. Bryanna tried everything to get me to eat."

"But every time you open your mouth, you think you'll choke." June spoke quietly. "I know the feeling."

"They said it was in my head. I told Bryanna I was suffocating. She thought I needed space. That was the one helpful suggestion she made. I quit therapy and moved out." Amelia glared at her. "What makes you think you know anything about it?"

June shook her head. "Just guessing." She passed Amelia the loaf of French bread. "Try this."

Amelia stopped slaughtering her lunch and broke off a piece. June carried their plates into the kitchen, scraping Amelia's uneaten portion into the trash. Ignoring the dishwasher, she ran a sinkful of suds, then stacked the clean dishes on the drainboard. Back in the living room, Amelia was leafing through a magazine and sipping bottled water. June carried her ginseng to the couch.

Amelia said, "I can't believe you're really drinking that stuff."

She swallowed thoughtfully. "I think it's an acquired taste. It kind of grows on you."

Amelia continued to read, ignoring her. June took the magazine.

"Hey."

"Time to talk."

"I didn't eat. I don't owe you anything."

"Is that how you think this works? Like some

kind of trade? I've got news for you. I don't care if you starve. But before you do, you're going to talk to me. Then you can get back to killing yourself and I can get back to work."

"Do you like what you do?" Amelia faced her. "Do you enjoy all this cloak-and-dagger stuff?"

June smiled. "You're hardly top secret."

"Oh, right. I'm just one of the boring details in a much more important case. Get fucked. Or go back to shooting terrorists or whatever the hell it is you do. Go negotiate somewhere else. I'm not talking to you."

"The thing is," June said softly, "I can eat. I'm just afraid to breathe."

Amelia didn't move. "Why?"

Because the air was full of fire, and if she inhaled, flames would sear her throat and fill her lungs. Hot air would expand in her chest until her rib cage exploded. Because if she opened her mouth, the flames that already raged inside would come pouring out.

Amelia wasn't the only one who needed a good therapist.

"Here's the deal," June said. "You tell me your story, unedited, start to finish. Then I'll tell you mine."

"How do I know it'll be good?"

"Because I know what it feels like to kill someone. Do you?"

"I didn't kill him," Amelia whispered. "But I'm glad he's dead." Her lips barely moved. "He'd gotten up — I thought he was going to leave." She closed her eyes. "He kicked me." Her shoulders shook but no tears escaped. "I was swallowing so much blood I couldn't breathe." Her chest heaved. She grabbed a shirt from the laundry pile and scrubbed her face. She wasn't crying. She said flatly, "He kicked me like he wanted to kill me. Then something exploded. I felt the blood and I thought it was mine. I just couldn't feel any more pain."

"Who was it?" June asked gently. "Who did you see?"

She shook her head. "I didn't see anyone."

June spaced her questions, keeping her voice calm. "You told the police you saw a man."

"No. I couldn't see."

"I'm going to take you back for a minute. Stay with me, okay? You were at the bar." She waited for Amelia to nod. "When did you decide to leave?"

"I was with Bryanna. We were fighting and I left."

"By yourself?"

"Yes. No. You know this already. I was with Bryanna."

"You told the police that Bryanna left early. She confirmed the story."

"Don't talk like a cop."

"Bryanna said she left first and took the car home."

"I told her to say that."

June cursed silently. She didn't want Amelia's story to change. She wanted to find what everyone expected — nothing. Then she could fax her report to Colt and be done with it. Now Amelia was admitting she'd lied. She asked patiently, "Why did you say Bryanna left first?"

Amelia tugged her fingers through her hair. Wind had tangled the curls. "We had a fight. I didn't want to tell the cops, that's all."

"What were you fighting about?"

"I told her I was leaving her. I'd taken money out of our account for a deposit on my own place. I was going to tell her in the morning, after I'd signed a lease. She wouldn't have found out, but she went to an ATM and checked the balance. It was low. The thing about Bryanna is, she always wants to process. She wanted to go home and talk. I told her I'd get home by myself."

"Did you stay at the club after she left?"

"We walked out together."

"What time was that?"

"I don't know. We weren't there very long. Maybe it was ten-thirty. I told her to take the car. The subway was across the street."

"Did she follow you?"

The hesitation was barely perceptible. "No."

"You don't know that for sure, do you? She could have followed you."

"She said she didn't."

"Was Bryanna looking for you? After you were assaulted, did she find you in the alley?" Amelia shook her head. "Is that why you told her to lie, so the police wouldn't question her?" She didn't answer. "Does Bryanna carry a gun?"

"No."

June tried to brush aside sympathetic thoughts. She reminded herself that Amelia's new statement would require tedious legwork and headache-inducing paperwork. She tried to make herself believe that

Amelia Wright was a pain in the butt. It didn't work. Her next question was gentle.

"Has Bryanna ever tried to hurt you?" Amelia wouldn't meet her eyes. She asked more firmly, "Would she harm you to stop you from leaving?" Amelia surged off the couch and kicked a coil of rope. June stood up. "Who are you protecting?"

"No one."

"You think Bryanna did it."

"I know she didn't."

"You told the police you saw a man. The truth is, you saw a woman. Was it Bryanna?"

"Cut it out." Amelia pushed past her and sank into the cushions, pulling her knees to her chin. "I told you, I didn't see anyone."

June looked down. Amelia had been lying on the ground, her nose broken, ribs cracked, her body battered and raped. Her face had been hit so hard that both eyes had turned black and blue. Broken noses always bled like hell. Choking, blood in her throat, a booted foot assailing her chest. Then a shot. Pain eased. She arched, gasping, mouth open, swollen eyes closed.

I didn't see anyone.

June stared at her. "Amelia, what did you hear?"

The whisper was muffled by her knees. "I heard a woman."

Chapter 5

Bryanna Waters, née Beth Watkins, had changed her name more often than most people changed credit cards. June flipped through the file. Rainwater, Raindancer and Waterspirit were a few of the mailing label selections. She'd settled on Waters when she opened the chiropractic business. Nothing like an urge to make money to normalize personal image.

The office was in Jamaica Plain, not far from where Bryanna and Amelia had shared a house. The one-time lesbian ghetto was now part of the neighborhood crime-watch program. On weekdays, double-income dykes hustled toddlers to daycare, their Subarus full of car seats, juice boxes and Lesléa Newman stories. In front of a clapboard house, a hand-painted shingle announced Dr. Waters, as well as a naturopathic doctor and a massage therapist. Chimes sounded as she entered.

A cherubic woman with a pixie haircut looked up from an appointment book. "I'm sorry, we close early on Saturday. Can I schedule you for next week?"

"Bryanna Waters?"

"I'm Dr. Waters. And you are —?"

"Special Agent June Gavin. May we talk?"

The angelic face flushed. "Is this about Amelia? Is she all right?" Plump fingers curled around the phone.

"Dr. Waters, do you have an office where we can speak privately?"

"Oh. Um, right this way." She wore balloon pants with drawstrings at the waist and ankles. Birkenstock sandals did nothing to add height. "We share everything," Bryanna explained. "Private offices encourage power dynamics. We can talk in here." She ushered June into a treatment room and wrapped her legs around an ergonomic chair.

June looked in vain for a straight-backed chair, then settled her hip on the padded table. "Dr. Waters, two months ago, you lied to the police. Before I decide whether to file an obstruction charge, I'm going to give you a chance to amend your story. This is a good time to tell the truth."

Once more, round cheeks flushed. The dimpled chin started to quiver, and Bryanna Waters began to cry. "I'm so sorry." She located a tissue in her voluminous pants. "I told Amelia not to lie." She blew her nose. "I'm so relieved I can finally stop cording this event."

"I beg your pardon?"

"Cording the lie. It ties me energetically to the past. Now I can release it and move on. I told Amelia, for the sake of her own healing, she has to stop keeping secrets. That's why she can't eat, you know. She's stuffing such a big secret it fills her up inside."

June tried to count to ten. She got to two. "What secret is that?"

"That's just it." Bryanna pouted. "I don't know."

"Amelia lied so the police wouldn't question you. She's convinced you know everything." It was a cop trick, and Amelia would have called her on it. Bryanna wasn't so savvy.

"Oh, no," she said with a gasp. "No wonder we can't connect. If she thinks I'm hiding something . . . oh, this is awful." She dabbed her nose.

"Did you follow her to the subway?"

Tears glimmered and threatened to drip. "I begged her to come home and talk but she insisted on being alone." Wet eyes were earnest. "I would never violate her personal space."

"What if she were in danger? Would you go after her, try to help?"

"Yes, of course, if I knew that she needed my help."

"There are no limits to helping someone you love, isn't that so?"

"Love is unconditional."

"So if you had to hurt someone, even kill someone, to save her, you'd do it."

Bryanna said coldly, "I don't condone violence."

June softened her tone. "Dr. Waters, it's normal for citizens to want to protect themselves and the people they love. Lots of women make the decision to carry handguns."

Bryanna was indignant. "I support gun control. And I have a whistle on my key ring. It's very loud."

Bully for you. June bit her tongue. "So when you found Amelia in the alley, you tried to save her, then you ran for help."

"No, no. I wasn't in the alley. Oh, Amelia must be so angry. I would have gone with her, if she'd only asked."

"Dr. Waters, lying to the police is a serious offense." The tears were on the brink again. "Just tell me why you lied."

"Trust." Her chin lifted bravely. "Amelia told me to say I'd gone home early. She thought it would make things easier. She was so fragile, and I wanted her to know that she could trust me in every way."

"Did you think that if you lied for her she'd stay with you?"

"She did stay," Bryanna whispered. "For a while."

Eight weeks, June thought. Enough time for bruises to fade and bones to knit. Before leaving on her rafting trip, Amelia had moved into Marj's cottage.

"Thank you for your time, Dr. Waters. I'm sure, in the future, you'll be completely forthright with the authorities."

Bryanna nodded, eyes wet and wide. Then the floodgates collapsed. June exited quickly, trying to ignore the tearful sound of fresh healing.

* * * * *

She spent Sunday at the Fort Devens shooting range. There was a message from Bass when she got home. "Come up for clams."

She dialed his number and he answered on the seventh ring. She said, "Get a machine."

"Is that you, sure-shot?"

"I'm not with HRT anymore. Stop calling me that."

"You didn't talk to me for six years, now you're bitching like my ex."

"You should have taken her for clams while you had the chance."

"I did. On our twenty-second anniversary. She had the shits for three days. She cleaned out the medicine cabinet when she moved but she didn't take the Pepto-Bismol. Go figure. What'd you do to yours?"

"Gee, Bass, I'd love to talk, but this line isn't secure."

"Why do you think I'm asking you out? You sure as hell aren't my type."

"I'm gonna hang up now, before we both regret this phone call."

"How do you like working with Isaacs? Storky son-of-a-fish. He played college ball, you know. Indiana. Been in Boston for a year. Al Rahman's kind of an odd duck. I thought he'd retire from head-quarters. Or white collar, at least. I never figured that minnow for bank robbery."

Talking to Bass made her feel like she was lost at the zoo. Or an aquarium. "Have you satisfied your carnal curiosity about my co-workers?"

"Onion rings. Did I mention that? There's a place I know where you can watch the lobster boats. They dip the onions in beer-and-cornmeal batter. Sam

Adams beer. You gotta do it. It's your patriotic duty."
Her ears began to buzz. "Did you hear me?"

"Yeah." It was one of the oldest codes between them.

"So it's a date?"

"Yeah." She hesitated. "I'm working a case."

"Take a lunch break. Any day this week."

She hung up the phone and looked in the refrigerator. The housekeeper had a penchant for casseroles. She left the tuna noodles covered and pulled an alfredo sauce out of the freezer. She set pasta to boil and put on her bathrobe. By the time she'd finished eating, it was dark outside. She drew the curtain and left the lights off. Then she lay on the floor and unplugged the phone. The console was molded plastic, the answering tape built-in. She unscrewed the jack. Innocent wires stared back.

She lay on cinder block until her legs went numb, then he made her lie in the swamp, so she was numb and wet. She never knew when the signal would come. After one hour, or half a day. She lay relaxed, watchful, staring through her scope, eyes focused on target.

"Lie and watch," he said. "If the signal comes, shoot. Until then, keep watching. That's your patriotic duty."

Bass had called to warn her. Someone was watching. She got up from the floor and turned on a light. She flipped to the first movie she found on TV, stared at the screen until a decent interval had passed, then went to bed. When she awakened at three a.m., the apartment was empty. She sat in darkness and stared out the window. She didn't know who wanted her, or why.

On Monday morning, June announced herself at *Outdoors Woman*. The Boylston Street building had its own courtyard. Women in short skirts and running shoes crossed the marble foyer soundlessly; June's heels echoed. The men wore double-breasted suits and sunglasses. Dark-jacketed guards posed like statues next to decorative urns. Long-stemmed birds-of-paradise matched the patterned tile. On every level, the names of investment firms filled the directory. *Outdoors Woman* had offices on the twenty-fourth floor.

Windows overlooked a gothic church, the Copley Square fountains and the Prudential tower. Magazine staff, dedicated to deadlines, kept their hands on their keyboards, their backs to the view. The receptionist frowned, but June wasn't kept waiting.

"Ms. Gavin? Ms. MacMichael will see you now." The executive assistant's stiletto heels impaled the plush carpeting.

If manicures and fashion accessories were any indication, not everyone at *Outdoors Woman* was a camper. June followed a wafting trail of perfume into the editor's office. The assistant picked up computer disks and showed herself out.

"Killer scent. Never fails to ruin my breakfast.

I'm Marj MacMichael." A danish topped a pile of papers. Behind it, a robust woman in a tailored suit extended a hand. Two computer screens vied for her attention. In a corner, a fax machine hummed tunelessly. She moved to a sidebar. "Coffee? No? I'm having some. How about tea? It only takes a second to brew a pot."

"You brew fresh?"

"Of course. Why should tea drinkers suffer?"

"I'd love tea. Thank you."

Marj pressed an intercom. "Tea. While you're at it, bring Amelia's itinerary and hold my calls." She waved her to a seat. "So, Special Agent Gavin, may I call you June? Please tell me why you've been harassing my favorite, albeit slightly off-kilter, star writer. I'm warning you, if you mess with her writing, you're messing with me. Ah, here's your tea."

A knock at the door preceded the aroma of Darjeeling and another blast of perfume.

"I can't tell you how many hints I've dropped about a scent-free environment," Marj said when the door had closed. "Some Monday morning when I'm PMS, I'm going to fire her just because I can't stand the way she smells. I hope I don't. She's the only one who can read my calendar." She returned June's assessing gaze. "Amelia spent an hour on the phone Saturday night spitting bullets into my ear. You're better than the Buicks, but only slightly. Before we further abuse her privacy, why don't you tell me what you're after?"

"Two months ago, on the night Amelia was raped, Boston Consumer's Mutual noted an unauthorized transfer of funds. Recently, a vice president from that bank was abducted. The FBI is investigating the robbery and kidnapping."

"And Amelia is of interest to you ... why?"

"The person who shot her rapist may have robbed the bank."

"You mean the Good Sam shooter. He's a bank robber, too? This guy had a busy night."

"We're concerned about possible contact between Amelia and Good Sam. That was the reason for the initial investigation."

"Investigation? Is that a euphemism for harassment and emotional abuse? You people." Marj shook her head. "You walk all over civil rights, just because you think it's fun to play with phone taps. You did use a tap?"

"As I explained to Amelia, it's standard —"

"Save it." Marj waved her to silence. "Save it for someone who believes it. I certainly don't, and if you do, I'll be disappointed." She picked up her coffee. "Two months makes for old news. Why are you here now?"

"We're reviewing everything that happened in March."

"You're opening up old leads. I assume that means you have no new ones?"

June let a smile reach her lips. "Let's just say I've been assigned to the old-lead side of the case."

"Tell me you have new information. Otherwise, I'll ask you to leave."

"Amelia admitted that she lied to the police. Bryanna Waters also lied."

"Bryanna." Marj snorted. "Thank God Amelia finally dropped that ditz. Selfish as it sounds, I'd rather see her lonely than have to suffer through another office party with Dr. Waters in attendance."

June sipped her tea. It was strong and hot. She was beginning to like Marj MacMichael. "Do you know why Amelia lied?"

"I don't know what she lied about. How can I guess at the motivation?"

"Amelia trusts you, doesn't she?"

"Yes. A trust that's wearing thin, thanks to you."

"Does she confide in you?"

Marj sighed. "I wish she did. No, the truth is, when she's on deadline, I'm just as glad she keeps her thoughts to herself and gets her words on disk. But . . . something's been bothering her. I noticed it even before the rape, otherwise I'd blame it on the aftermath, PTSD. I've been . . . concerned."

"Please tell me why."

Marj poured herself more coffee. "Amelia's an excellent writer. She takes her readers right to the edge, then a little over. Our readership thrives on excitement. We cater to the weekend warriors and some serious athletes. They like to think they go all the way, every time. That's what Amelia does — she makes her readers believe in ultimate experience. But she's professional." She glanced out the window. "If I thought she was unsafe, I'd yank her out of the field faster than you can snap Spandex. She has beautiful instincts, knows just how far to take a story." She looked at June. "Lately, she's been going a little further." She handed her the folder left by the perfumed assistant. "She leaves tomorrow for San Diego. You'll want to talk to BJ, too." She stood. "By the way, what did she lie about?"

"The night she was raped, she didn't see a man. She heard a woman."

"I'll be damned." Marj looked delighted. "Good Sam is a girl."

"Any idea who she might be?"

"None at all. But when you find her, let me know. I'd like to pin a medal on her breast."

Cambridge was known for its crowded but distinctive neighborhoods. Painted trim ranged from gray to vivid lavender. BJ Honda's home stood apart by virtue of garden greenery. A brick path directed guests to the front door, then curved to a small backyard. Circular beds were planted with daffodils and tulips. Shade trees were showing green but the new growth was still thin. June's eyes were drawn to herb pots and window boxes. She climbed the porch and bent to take a leaf between her fingers, rubbing the velvety texture. She held her fingers to her nose and smiled. BJ was growing scented geraniums. One plant smelled like lemon, another like mint. The front door stood ajar, the entrance blocked by a screen. She rang the bell.

A voice called, "Out back. Come around."

The path slipped between two slender trees. She had to duck beneath a spray of blossoms — pink and white petals spilled like fountain water. Her eyes burned and her throat began to close. She stepped quickly through the offending boughs and sneezed. She had a vague impression of a dark-haired man and more droopy green things. Then her eyes swelled shut and she gasped.

A cheerful baritone said, "Beautiful, aren't they? Those are weeping cherry trees. Come inside." A hand pressed between her shoulder blades. "Three steps up. Now one more." The breeze disappeared, replaced by interior shadows. Chair legs scraped.

She fumbled to sit down. "Antihistamines. I'll take whatever you've got."

"This is better for you." Liquid gurgled.

She peered through streaming eyes and asked hopefully, "Alka-Seltzer?"

"Beet juice and cayenne pepper. Drink it."

She took a gulp. It soothed her throat but the aftertaste burned. She tried another swallow and her sinuses began to drain.

"Have a tissue." The deep voice joined itself to broad shoulders and a muscular chest. Full lips smiled under beautiful eyes. "Feeling better?"

She blew her nose. "God, that's worse than the ginseng."

BJ laughed. "I'm surprised Amelia let you stay long enough for a drink."

"She thinks she's poisoning me with your home brew." She cleared her throat. "I'm not usually so bad this early in the season. What are you growing?"

"I'm repotting herbs but that's not what's bothering you. My retired neighbor mows his dime-store lawn every other day. He uses a gas-powered mower and chemical weed-killer. I want you to arrest him."

"Sorry, that's out of my jurisdiction. I take it you know who I am?"

"Marj called ten minutes ago with instructions to cooperate. She thinks if we're helpful, you'll go easy on Amelia."

"There's nothing easy or hard about it. I ask questions. Either you know the answers or you don't." She blew her nose again.

"Ah, the Zen of true and false." He joined her at the table. "But everyone perceives truth differently, based on their own experience. Have you ever studied Zen, Agent Gavin?"

"No."

"Are you sure?" He left the kitchen and returned with sheets of fax paper. "We have access to a lot of archives." He sounded apologetic. "Marj thought this article was interesting."

She stared at the familiar news story. The Bureau's image-makers had milked the event. The words *heroic sharpshooter* had been underscored, along with her name. She pushed it away. "That was a long time ago."

"It takes incredible focus, doesn't it? To be such a good shot, you have to concentrate, and practice. Meditation is like that. But Zen practice is supposed to bring peace of mind. How do you find peace after killing someone?"

She rested her elbows on the table. "You don't like what I do for a living? Get in line. Why don't you take your boss's advice and cooperate?"

"She thinks you're sympathetic because you're female. Don't prove her wrong. Marj doesn't like to be crossed."

"I don't work for Marj." She waited for his smile to fade. "How long have you and Amelia been working together?"

He folded his arms. "Two years, on and off."

"Are you going to San Diego?"

"Nope. That's girls only. No boy-kittens allowed. I'm going birding in North Carolina."

"Bird-watching? Isn't that a little tame for *Outdoors Woman*?"

"We fly to and from the nature reserve by hot air balloon."

"Oh. How well do you know Bryanna?"

"Better than I'd like to, frankly. None of Amelia's friends could stand her. They met because Bryanna was tagging along after the softball team. After they hooked up, Amelia stopped seeing her old crowd. Now she isolates herself completely."

"Did she talk to you about the rape?"

"She doesn't talk to anyone."

"She was in counseling."

"Sure, if that's what you call two sessions. Therapy was Bryanna's idea. If Amelia wants to sort something out, she'll do it on top of a mountain. Talking isn't her style. Can I get you some more beet juice?"

"No, thanks."

He balanced his chair on two legs, arms still locked across his chest. "After she was raped, I wanted her to stay with me. But she didn't have the strength to fight Bryanna. Bryanna loved taking care of Amelia." He frowned. "Too much."

"Did Amelia tell you she was planning the break-up?"

"Not in so many words. I sensed it, though. When she starts throwing herself out of airplanes and dangling from cliffs, something's up."

"Isn't that her job?"

"There's work and there's insanity. She's been

camped on the edge for a while. That's why I thought her love life might be in trouble. But Bryanna's the one who gave me the news flash. She came over after she left the bar. While Amelia was being brutalized, Bryanna was sobbing on my shoulder."

She held his gaze. "They both lied to the police."

He shrugged. "Bryanna's reality is a little warped."

"They walked out of the bar together. They were fighting."

"She shouldn't have left her alone." His voice was full of quiet venom. "Do you want to do something useful? See to it that every damp, ugly alley in this cruel city is bricked up, and arrest all the homophobes. While you're at it, shut down the hetero weight rooms. Amelia was raped by a boxer on a steroid overdose. I guess he got himself pumped up pretty good and decided he didn't want to do himself."

June waited for his anger to abate. She'd read the police and autopsy reports. Amelia's rapist had weighed two hundred and forty-five pounds. She asked, "When Bryanna was here, what did she talk about?"

"Love and understanding. She didn't think she was getting her fair share. And she was sniveling about some trip they'd planned and never got to take. A spiritual mountain hideaway. Rock climbing and crystals. No wonder that relationship never worked."

"When did you find out about the assault?"

"Marj called. Amelia's estranged from her family. Talk about homophobic. It kind of sucks when your employer is the person to notify. She was in the hospital overnight, then Bryanna took her home. The bitch of it is, she was probably on her way over here. Bryanna knew it, too. She was crying her eyes out, waiting to see if Amelia would show."

"Did Bryanna go into the alley?"

He looked incredulous. "You think she watched her lover get raped, drove away, then watered my shirt like I'm ivy? Oh, and killed the rapist, with a gun that no one knows she has."

"Did she?"

"You're really groping under skirts."

"Did Bryanna and Amelia fight a lot?"

"They broke up. Have you met Bryanna? How long do you think you'd last?"

"Were there signs of abuse?"

"You're getting offensive."

"Physical abuse," she snapped. "Did it happen?"

His eyes were black ice. Slowly, the edges melted. "I never saw it," he said softly. "I think I would have." He swore under his breath.

"Do you know any women who might have been in the alley that night? Someone Amelia knows or wants to protect?"

"First Bryanna, now women in general?"

"The person who shot Amelia's rapist was probably a woman."

"In that case, there was a bar full of lesbians across the street. Haven't you come up with the man-hating killer-dyke motive yet?"

"Be specific. Who had a motive?"

His chair tipped back to earth. "Besides Bryanna, I don't know who Amelia was seeing." Pain etched his expressive face. "I was hoping the snow fountain cherries would be in bloom this month. The weeping cherry trees in the backyard," he explained. "They're right on schedule."

"On schedule for what, BJ?"

"Didn't anyone tell you? Amelia and Bryanna. They were going to get married."

Chapter 6

June rode an empty elevator to the seventh floor. In the late afternoon, the corridors were quiet, and her desk, thankfully, was free of Al's paperwork. She logged onto the shared computer terminal and scrolled through her e-mail. Nothing but routine memos — an admonishment from public relations against agents making press statements, and a reminder to attend a handgun safety seminar. She was about to delete the seminar notice, when a line of type caught her eye.

"Be safe. Don't sacrifice accuracy. Close the gaps in training."

She remembered Bass watching her practice. "Don't ever try to teach a recruit how to shoot."

"Why not?"

"You shift your focus between the target and sights. That's not the way we train."

She lowered the Browning. "I thought you wanted accuracy."

"No one shoots the way you do. Even snipers rely too much on their scopes. In the dark, in a shoot-out, I tell field agents to keep the barrel level."

"That goes without saying."

He spat. "You're naïve. You think you're always gonna have all the time in the world to take aim."

"If I can't see the gap, I won't take the shot." The statement slipped out before she realized it sounded childish.

He didn't answer right away. Finally, he asked, "What's the most important thing in target shooting?"

"The gap."

He shook his head. "You've been staring at paper for too long. The most important thing is the target. Make sure you've got the right one." He laughed. "I guess we could call that a gap in your knowledge."

He put her through the multiple targets course and taught her to choose. If she took too long, he said, "Close the gap."

* * * * *

The message was from Bass again. He wanted to see her. He was telling her it couldn't wait. She deleted the memo. She'd make a report to Shane, then drive to Portsmouth. She'd find an excuse.

Opening a document file, she began typing her interview notes. She referred to the police report. With the rapist dead, there'd been little investigative follow-up, and only cursory interviews with the women at the bar. Amelia's assertion that she'd seen a man had been taken at face value. The press had loved Good Sam. No one had faulted the police for not making an arrest.

She double-checked, but she already knew that neither Amelia nor Bryanna was a licensed handgun owner. She tossed the print-outs aside. Could Bryanna have shot the rapist, left Amelia, called 911 and then gone crying to BJ? Implausible. She flipped back a page. The 911 call had come from the bar. A man at a lesbian club would draw notice. But what better place for a woman to hide? She glanced at her clothes. Pressed slacks and a jacket. Shit. She hated the bar scene. She didn't have anything to wear.

"How's it going?" Shane propped himself in the entrance to her cubicle. His spaghetti-thin body looked like it didn't have enough starch to stand upright. He clasped one knee, balancing like a bland flamingo.

"Wright lied about the gunman. Good Sam is female. She also lied when she said she left the club alone. She was with her girlfriend, Bryanna Waters, and they were fighting. Wright had tried to break it off. Waters paid a visit to a friend, and then went home."

"What's your take on the girlfriend? Is this domestic?"

"Hard to say. Waters says she wasn't anywhere near the alley. She believes in . . . space. The nine-one-one call came from the club."

"Did you do the bar scene yet?"

"Tonight."

"Okay. I'll notify Colt. Get a report on my desk in the morning."

"Where do we stand with the kidnap investigation?"

"Colt's handling it. Gavin, stay focused on Good Sam. If there's something there that Colt can use, let's give it to him. Share some notes with Al," he suggested. "You can learn a lot from him."

She said, "Have you noticed that Al doesn't like to share?" Shane was staring at her. She asked, "What?"

"Nothing." He smirked. "I was just wondering what you were going to wear tonight." He sauntered out.

Bass, she reflected, hadn't limited his gossip to nicknames. It was time for a visit. She'd even let him buy her a beer. In a bottle, so she could crack his head with it.

The bar was closed on Monday night and wouldn't open again until midweek. First thing on Tuesday morning, June e-mailed her preliminary report to Shane. There was a message notifying her of a meeting with Colt that afternoon. She checked her watch. She could be in Portsmouth in an hour. She got in the Porsche and headed north, speeding.

She called Bass from her car phone and reached him at the resident agency.

"You know what the biggest tourist attraction in town is?" His voice crackled, then boomed. "Everyone watches the drawbridge. It's got bells and sirens like some kind of carnival ride. There's a floating restaurant in the marina where you can order a martini. Watching the bridge isn't as romantic as a sunset, but it goes up and down twice an hour."

She said, "I'll check it out."

The marina wasn't hard to find, although the shipboard restaurant wasn't open yet for business. June chose a bench near the water where she had a view of the bridge. Traffic flowed over it while the current streamed smoothly under. She'd been waiting for about ten minutes when Bass joined her. He was carrying two covered paper cups and handed her one. She opened it and sniffed appreciatively.

"Thanks, Bass."

"They shipped that tea from India this morning. From the boat to your cup. That's how fresh it is." He was sipping cappuccino. "How's the caseload? Are your sea legs back?"

"I never lost the feel for it," she said softly.

He took off his sunglasses. "It's worse, isn't it? To have it and not use it. Especially when you know it's there." He gazed over the water. "Putting someone like you behind a desk is like trying to stuff a full-sized tree into an ornamental planter. No way is that going to fit."

"I had nightmares." She kept it in the past tense. "I never told anyone."

He chuckled. "Maybe when I'm dead and cremated I won't have bad dreams. You know why we don't talk about it? We don't want to bring it home. We don't want the filth to touch our families. We act like it's something we leave behind, like dog crap you scrape off your shoe. Then one day your wife looks at you and says, 'Buster, you stink.' " He clapped her on the knee and put his sunglasses back on. "Headquarters is taking notes on you. I don't know why."

She sipped tea, letting the steam soothe her dry throat. "What do you know, Bass?"

"Are you solo, or did Shane set you up to work with Al Rahman?"

"Al's taken over my desk space, but he won't let me touch anything. We aren't exactly sharing case notes."

Bass grunted. "Just as well."

She watched him and waited. *Don't just go fishing,"* he used to say. *"When you cast, expect a strike."*

Finally he said, "Rahman didn't officially transfer to Boston. Technically, he's still based at headquarters. That's all I know."

June said, "The case I'm on is being supervised by a division assistant director. What can you tell me about Edward Colt?"

"If Colt's in charge, then Rahman may be one of his precautions. I hate it when they work that way."

Bass never taught his trainees to fight fair. But using one agent to spy on another went against his grain.

She asked, "Are you going to retire up here?"

He shrugged. "Why not? The fishing's good."

"You belong at Quantico."

He didn't answer right away. When he did, his voice was low. "I'm the last person I figured for a scenic relocation." He studied the current. "You know what I hate more than bad weather? People who grumble about it."

"Did you invite Brenda to come for a visit?" She indicated the marina restaurant. "Order lobster. Skip the clams."

He laughed. "Yeah, sure. I'll ask my estranged wife on a date. Good idea."

She regarded him. He was a smart, caring man. On the way to Portsmouth she'd played his Elvis Costello tape, and guessed that when his wife left he'd listened to "A Good Year for the Roses," and probably cried.

She said, "Keep your hooks clear of headquarters, Bass. From what I've seen of Colt, he's not going to want a supervisory senior snooping in his cases. Even if you are a legend in your own time."

"Make sure your work is clean. Spic and span." He stood and tossed his coffee cup in the trash.

Just then a siren sounded and lights on the drawbridge began to flash. When the traffic had cleared, weighted pulleys descended and the center section of the bridge rose smoothly.

"What'd I tell you?" Bass said. "A fucking carnival ride. See you, Gavin. You owe me a beer."

"Call Brenda," she yelled after him.

That afternoon, Edward Colt was back at the Boston field office.

"Conference room," Shane said.

June asked, "Is Al on the case?"

"He's investigating the armored car holdups in Framingham. Feel free to share notes, though."

"Gavin." Colt nodded as June walked in and took a seat at the table. "Good work on your initial report."

"Thank you, sir."

"It makes our job easier, now that we know Good Sam's a girl."

"With respect, sir, the only information that's come to light is Good Sam's gender. There's no hard evidence that Good Sam was in the bank. Just the time on the computer log, and the nine-one-one call. And I can't see any connection to the kidnapping."

Colt tapped the table. "The key with this case is that the robbery came first."

"Let's go with the theory that Good Sam robbed the bank," Shane said. "All the robberies are done by stealing access codes and creating user IDs. But Boston's different because she started from inside. She robbed them on location, then the vice president was nabbed."

"Two months later," June said. "Why the time lag?"

"Good Sam isn't part of the kidnap operation." Colt was adamant. "She's competing with them, trying to mess them up. That's why she's so valuable. If we can get her, she'll give us the kidnappers."

"If that's true," Shane said, "then the kidnappers probably want Good Sam as much as we do."

Colt's urgency was palpable. "It's been five days since the banker was abducted. Keep the momentum going. Get me Good Sam."

June asked, "Has there been any progress with the hostage negotiations?"

Colt's face closed. He had square features and deeply set eyes. His hair was thick and dark. She wondered if he colored it. He was still a handsome man, although no longer lean. At the moment, fatigue marred his powerful edge. He looked puffy around the eyes and under his chin. He fiddled with the ring on his right hand, twisting the band.

He said, "There are no negotiations."

"They broke down?" Shane asked.

"They were never initiated."

"A ransom demand was made," June said.

"The first and only message received from the kidnappers gave a ransom amount that matched the robbery amount. That's how we know who we're dealing with. They wanted us to know."

"Nothing else?"

"There's been no further contact."

June couldn't believe it. "That's absurd."

Colt said, "They're not in it for the money this time. They're after Good Sam."

"With this kind of rivalry," Shane said, "I wouldn't be surprised if Good Sam is a spinoff from the kidnappers. It feels like bad blood."

Colt's skin looked gray, and June wondered at the emotions weighing on him. The rigors of the case, probably. He was responsible for a kidnap victim whose captors weren't talking. Without dialogue, chances were the abducted bank vice president was already dead. She felt some sympathy for Edward Colt.

She thought about this morning's conversation with Bass. Colt had checked her background before bringing her into the investigation. He'd made no secret of it — praising her father, commenting on her eyesight. A man like Colt would want to know everything about the people who worked for him. But had he brought in Al Rahman to dig further, to keep tabs on her? Surely she didn't rate so much attention. She wondered if Shane knew what Al was up to, and if he approved.

Colt brought her back to the moment. "You haven't done follow-up interviews at the bar. Why?"

"The establishment reopens tomorrow."

Colt stood. "Update me daily, at least by e-mail."

Shane stood up when Colt was gone; June stayed seated.

"Gavin? Is there something you want to add?"

She stared at Shane, then got to her feet. They were nearly eye-to-eye. He didn't blink. After a moment, she said, "No, sir."

Part II
AMELIA WRIGHT

Chapter 7

Amelia was trying to pack. Later that night, she'd be on the red-eye to San Diego. Tomorrow morning, she'd be sailing.

She stood in the center of the cottage and surveyed a mess of camping gear. She'd given fleeting consideration to building basement shelves. She didn't think Marj would mind. She doubted if Marj would notice. Her editor wasn't the basement-project type. The problem with shelves was that they signified permanence. Marj hadn't given any indication that she wanted her beach house back. But warm weather was on its way. Vacation crowds would settle in — pale-faced New Englanders scouring the shores, searching for tans. With chairs and coolers, chatter and aluminum cans, they'd lose watches and spare change to the beachcombers. She didn't know if she belonged. She wanted a sign, something tangible, like the stakes the homesteaders had pounded.

The only place she couldn't live was Cincinnati. Years ago, she'd realized that living with her family was the worst thing in the world. Having decided that simple fact, she'd dismantled and packed her bicycle and boarded a bus. She'd had to live in California for a year to get financial aid. Before she graduated, she'd gone back for Christmas break and found a Bible on her bed and a brand new picture of Jesus over the television.

A new cross-stitch hung in the kitchen, made in honor of her homecoming. "Love the sinner." She stared at it through a silent dinner, analyzed the pattern of green and yellow x's. A sickly vine uplifted the tormenting words. They were familiar words, flung at her since she'd been sent home from high school, suspended. A football player had found her, nestled with a cheerleader in the unmown grass behind the equipment shed. Practice was long over. The boy had followed them.

"What did you do to that innocent girl?" The family minister assumed it was Amelia's fault. The cheerleader had long hair and wore a pleated skirt.

"I held her hand."

"You tried to seduce her."

"We were just talking."

When he began quoting Scripture, she stopped listening. He prayed for her soul. She wished he'd shut up. She'd never repented. It was a standoff to the end between the Baptist and the baby dyke.

Coming home had been a mistake. Amelia force-fed herself one overcooked pork chop and then threw up quietly in the bathroom. She brushed the taste of vomit and mushroom soup out of her mouth, then checked the Trailways schedule for the next departing bus. She didn't touch her bed or the Bible. At the front door, she looked back.

Her father was one year away from his pension, less than two years from a heart attack. Even if she'd known he was going to die, she wouldn't have stayed. In a corner of her mind, he was still watching the news, refusing to lift his eyes when she opened the door.

When her mother looked up, her heart surged, then hope drained like gravy through a sieve. She shook herself free of the sentimental clumps.

Her mother's glance swept over her, glassy and cold. It fixed on the clock. "I'll put up some jelly now, for the Christmas baskets."

She had left before her mother got out of her chair.

She kicked a climbing rope out of the way and emptied a suitcase. Summer clothes. The furniture's pastel fabric disappeared under an assortment of neon sport bras. She wasn't ready for summer. She turned to look at the view. Sometimes all she saw was sand; sometimes the ocean engulfed the glass. Now the sky swept in and pushed aside the waves. She returned to her task, choosing shorts and T-shirts. She dumped the rest of the pile on the floor. Then, because her packing was incomplete, she hurled the suitcase at the basement door.

* * * * *

Bryanna had been bent over the hospital bed. "You poor baby." When Bryanna tried to take her hand, Amelia flinched. Bryanna's eyes darkened. "I'm taking you home."

The doctor assessed the damage. Her nose was broken but it would heal. Not perfectly, but she said no to plastic surgery. Bryanna held the ice pack over one swollen eye, then the other. Her sternum was bruised, ribs cracked.

"It's going to hurt like hell to breathe," the doctor said.

Resignation knotted around her like an extra bandage while Bryanna did the grocery shopping, prepared soup and packaged plastic baggies full of ice. They didn't talk about the break-up. When she could bear the strain, she began lifting weights. Lying on a mat, she pushed a little harder, lifted a little more. And remembered the weight of a man on top of her. Intercostal muscles shrieked and she let them. She didn't expect to get raped again. Weight-lifting wasn't prevention — it was a penance. Because she'd lost. It didn't matter that the winner was dead. The only thing that mattered was endurance.

"Depression," the therapist said.

It was a huge, meaningless word. Everyone assumed, because she couldn't eat, because she no longer bothered with friends and shared meals, because she shunned the entertaining and mundane details of life, that she was empty. She tried to explain, made an effort to describe the pressure under her lungs. The therapist listened and nodded, gave an encouraging smile. When the clueless empathy became unbearable, she stood by the window. In a panicked attempt to breathe, she threw it open. Finally, she'd climbed outside and lowered herself, window frame to window frame, three stories to the ground.

She left her packing and stared through the picture window. The trick was to stay outside.

Suni was on the dock, loading supplies. The writer almost escaped her notice but the camera caught her attention. It was the only expensive part of the outfit. She realized she'd been expecting Lycra and lipstick, a model, a personality to match the magazine. But the woman walking toward her had neither a model's glamour nor stature. She was average height, which made her inches taller than Suni, with brown hair that curled and tangled on her collar. Baggy shorts hung on her hips. A short-sleeved shirt, tied at the waist, looked a size too loose. A flashy windbreaker, a concession to fashion, draped the camera bag. But it was her stride that drew Suni's eye — each step full of tension, as though, like a gazelle, she might unleash a burst of speed.

The writer took off her sunglasses and held out her hand. "Suni Sula? I'm Amelia Wright, from

Outdoors Woman magazine." Suni reached tentatively, unsure how to greet her guest. "Our editor was intrigued by your press release, Ms. Sula. High Tide Adventures sounds like just the kind of company our readers love to discover."

"It's Suni. Both names are really a lot longer and unpronounceable." She finally took Amelia's hand. "I've read your articles," she admitted. "I wanted to meet you."

"Well, I hope you're not disappointed." Amelia smiled. "I'm no sailor."

"You will be. On my boats, everyone sails. If you don't know how, you'll learn."

"I'm looking forward to it."

Suni stared at the muscled arm under the camera bag. She hadn't really been waiting for a model. Amelia Wright was just what she'd been expecting.

Amelia dropped her duffel. At the last minute, BJ had come over to help her pack.

"You're going to need a new wardrobe," he'd warned.

"Get out of my face."

He ignored her, opening the bag she'd finally zipped shut. "No shortage of athletic brassieres," he observed.

"I mean it, BJ. I'm not in the mood."

"The only mood you've been in for months is grouchy." He held up a cotton T-shirt. "This will be absolutely useless when it's wet."

"Who cares? It fits."

He eyed her critically. "I'm going to feed you. How about a pizza before you catch your plane?"

"Take-out? You must be really worried." BJ opposed fast food on principle. Too much packaging was bad for the environment. "Okay. Pepperoni."

"Don't try my patience." He dumped the last of her clothes out of the bag. "Your FBI friend came to see me."

"She's not my friend."

"Maybe she'll take you shopping for some new clothes. Tailored blouses, creased slacks, tasteful, quiet colors. Very stylish. Then there's the leather pumps —"

"You're boring me. She looks like an advertisement for L.L. Bean."

"And you look like the poster child for the Hunger Project."

"Go get dinner."

He held up a bra, stretching the colorful fabric. "Why don't you give her some fashion tips? Give her a call, see if she wants to borrow some Spandex."

She pushed him toward the door. He came back with garlic pizza. They sat side by side and she watched, fascinated, while he consumed an aromatic slice. She swallowed a few bites, then closed the box. She leaned into him, not speaking. She envied him his size, his broad shoulders and gorgeous chest. He was an attractive man who never kept a relationship for more than nine months.

"It's the traveling," he said when she asked. "Men can't stand a partner who's gone three weekends a month. No one wants a part-time wife."

The traveling had driven Bryanna crazy. She'd

dealt with it by fussing. Chubby, energetic Bryanna, who'd brought home gourmet groceries and videos each evening. In the morning, she'd served bagels in bed. Comfortable Bryanna, who'd made them a home filled with good food and tenderness, until the tenderness began to smother. Telling Bryanna they were through was like tearing off a Band-Aid. The quicker the better.

"I know you don't love me the way I love you," she'd said that night.

Amelia looked into teary eyes. "I'm sorry. I know this hurts."

"We can do couples counseling."

"Let it go."

"I don't want to. I love you."

"I know. But I don't love you. I'm not . . . in love."

"You've lived with me for two years. What about the wedding?"

"I never should have agreed to that."

"I thought you liked being with me."

"You've been a good friend."

"Do you want to stay friends?"

Amelia stared at the table, then forced herself to meet Bryanna's gaze. "No."

Bryanna gasped, then bit her lip. "I'll take us home."

"Take the car. I can take the subway to BJ's. I'll move this weekend."

"Why are you doing this? Amelia, come home so we can talk. When you figure out what's really bothering you, you'll feel better. I'll make omelettes, baby, whatever you want."

"It won't work, Bry. I'm not hungry and I don't want to talk. I can't fall in love with you."

"I know, honey. I know you're not in love. It's okay. Isn't that what I always tell you? I don't mind."

And that's the problem, Amelia thought. You know I don't love you and you don't care. Breakfast wasn't going to help. She craved intimacy, the place under companionship where there was heartache, even anger. Something harder and deeper than comfort. And stronger.

She never made it to the subway. Bryanna came to the hospital, took her home and did everything to help her heal, at least on the outside. She'd given up hoping that Bryanna could touch more than skin.

Lying on the floor of her study, she did sit-ups until her abdomen rippled. When she could lift weights without screaming, she called Marj.

"I want an assignment."

"Are you ready to go back to work?"

"Just get me out of here."

"Pack up the Jeep. You can stay at my cottage."

"That's not far enough."

There was a pause while Marj weighed options. "Get your gear together. I'll call you back."

When the phone rang again, Marj said, "Whitewater rafting. BJ's going, too. Do you think you can handle it?"

On a river in Maine, she'd dug in her paddle and gone over a waterfall. Momentarily, when the raft left the earth, her body felt whole, and the ache in her lungs had eased, ever so slightly.

* * * * *

97

Amelia inhaled salty air and surveyed the docks. In San Diego, summer had long since arrived. Morning fog lingered, tangled in rigging, wrapped around empty masts. At their moorings, a line of boats lay placidly, sails furled. Water rippled and stilled, smooth as sunlight.

Suni said, "High Tide Adventures doesn't offer cruises. I take women-only crews on working voyages. Three or four days, up to two or three weeks. I can also charter longer trips." Amelia switched on a hand-held recorder. "I've got two boats. The larger one, *The Bengal*, is berthed near San Francisco. She's double-masted, a ketch, which gives a lot of versatility for ocean cruising. *The Bengal* can take a six-woman crew to Hawaii." She smiled. "We're not going to be quite so ambitious on this trip." She indicated a boat. "This is *Little Bengal*."

Amelia took in the tidy deck and tall mast. The boat sported a bright orange hull and wavy black stripes. "Nice paint job."

"I like it, too. She's a sloop, which means one mast with the jib forward of the mainsail." She pronounced it "mains'l." "The design makes her faster in the water but easier for a small crew to handle."

"What if you get an inexperienced group?"

"I teach them. The only thing I don't allow on my boats are sightseers. On this trip, we'll be sailing down the Baja peninsula."

Amelia clicked off the recorder. "Okay. Assume I'm a beginner. Show me the ropes."

"We'll start with knots."

She reminded her of BJ --- a tiny, feminine version. Her dark hair was shorter, just a tail on her neck. Muscles glided under burnished skin. Unlike BJ's open, teasing humor, her smile was private.

Standing on the docks, Amelia's energy returned. It was as if her corpuscles, sensing fresh air, had grabbed more oxygen. She grinned. "Show me everything."

Chapter 8

Suni was a practiced teacher, patient, encouraging, also challenging and smart. Amelia watched her quick fingers as she handled the rope — over, over, under; up, around and down. She pulled it tight, practicing a stop knot and a bowline.

"You've handled rope before."

Amelia nodded. "Climbing."

"You'll need the muscle." Suni stood up. "Okay. Let's learn the rigging." She moved lightly around the deck, pointing to stays and shrouds, explaining standing and running rigging. "Halyards are the lines that raise and lower the sails. Sheets let them in and out. We'll raise the mainsail first."

She showed her how to feed the sail onto the boom and insert the battens. When the halyard was attached, they raised the sail. The smaller jib was next.

"The lines are called sheets, and they run through leads, or pulleys," Suni said. "Tie a stop knot. Good. Does everything make sense so far?"

"It's like learning a foreign language."

"You'll get the hang of it. Let's stow your gear and take a practice run."

Below the hatchway, she pointed out the compact galley. "*Little Bengal* has an icebox and freshwater tanks, and we always carry dry stores. On this trip, we'll be in port at night. I hope you like fruit and fish." She indicated a work station. "Navigation. You'll learn the charts as we go."

Single berths were spaced aft, by the navigator's seat, and in the forepeak. A table, wide enough to seat four, folded into a double berth. Amelia's duffel fit into a locker under the bunks. She paused to caress the wood grain.

Suni smiled. "Pretty, isn't she? I had the bulkheads refinished with ash. The sole, which is what you're standing on, is the original teak and holly."

Amelia knelt. The cabin floor was glossed to a rich finish. Strips of dark teak alternated with very thin strips of light holly inlay. "It's beautiful."

Suni said, "Modern boats are beamier, with more headroom, but I like the slender, old-fashioned lines. Hang wet clothes in the head and we'll get along fine."

Back on deck, she jumped to the dock and

released the mooring line. Amelia held the jib sheet, the rope for the smaller sail.

Suni stepped up. "Get ready to back the jib. Let it out, that's right." As wind caught the sail, the bow of the boat began to turn. Suni guided the tiller, and the sloop nosed away from the dock. "Look at the telltales," she called. Amelia looked up to see bits of wool fluttering from the shrouds. "Tack describes the wind with respect to the sails," Suni said. "When we change tack downwind, that's called a jibe. I want you to trim the main on my command. Prepare to jibe!" Amelia began pulling in the mainsheet. "Jibe ho!" Suni called. She pushed the tiller and Amelia ducked under the swinging boom. The boat crossed the line of wind, and Amelia eased out the filling sail. Suni smiled. "Not bad. Let's do it again."

She tacked back and forth, and Amelia began to get a feel for the boat.

"You're sailing on a beam reach," Suni said, "with the wind at right angles to the boat. Watch what happens when we get closer to the wind." She pushed the tiller. "See how the sails luff?" Amelia pulled the sheets until the flapping stopped. "That's it. Ease the sail until it luffs, then trim it. When we're sailing as close to the wind as possible, we're close-hauled. Are you ready for a little excitement?"

"Anytime."

Suni nodded. "To sail upwind, we make a series of tacks. It's called beating. Uncleat the jib on my command. Ready about!" The force of the wind seemed to increase. Suni called, "Hard alee!" The headsail began to luff and Amelia hauled it in. The boom swung and she glanced back, saw a flash of a smile. "Keep it trim!" She braced as the keel lifted.

At Suni's command, *Little Bengal* tacked again, zig-zagging upwind. "Nicely done." The roar quieted. Suni said, "Come sit over here and take the tiller." Her hand covered Amelia's. It was an instructional gesture, imparting reassuring warmth before moving away. She explained the points of sail while Amelia practiced. "When you're close to the wind, there's a lot of sideways force on the sails, so the boat heels. Give it a try."

With the sails trimmed all the way in, wind pummeled them. The boat skimmed and heeled, hanging between the air and the tide. They sought open ocean and the docks disappeared. Amelia laughed and eased off, letting her shoulders relax. She lifted her face, enjoying the sun.

A sudden wave slapped the stern. She pushed the tiller, trying to compensate, and the jib went soft.

"Duck!" Suni yelled. The luffing jib crossed first, then the boom swung hard. Suni's hand was on hers, easing the tiller, calming the sails. The boat slowed, responding like a dancing partner to a graceful lead. "That's called a flying jibe. One of the best I've seen in a while."

"Sorry."

"Not at all. For a moment, you were sailing by-the-lee, with the wind on the same side as the boom. It's a little dangerous." She smiled. "You're getting better."

Amelia sailed until her muscles tensed and relaxed naturally, without conscious thought.

At Suni's nod, she hauled up. "Shift your weight," Suni called. "Keep it trim."

She held the sheets and braced her feet. Copying Suni, she raised her hips and leaned back. Beside her,

Suni was streamlined, perfectly balanced. She leaned
farther out, countering the straining sails, the wind
like a wall at her back. She lay in the air, suspended,
and the boat flew — a thin orange line between
shades of blue. Suni's smile was white sunshine.

They came down slowly. Suni slipped into the
boat, guiding the tiller. Weight returned.

"I want to do that again."

Suni laughed. "You're a natural. Sure, we'll do it
again. I promise." There was something in her voice.
Amelia looked up but wind scattered the sound. Suni
cleated the sails. "Back in a sec." She went below,
returning with cartons of juice. "I'm serving lemonade. Pink or yellow, take your pick."

"Anything. Thanks." She tipped her head for a
long swallow and her eyes began to tear. She pulled
off her sunglasses, blinking to clear the glare. "That's
really good." She wiped her mouth. "What do you do
if your sailors don't like lemons?"

"I had a crew once that showed up with a full
mini-bar. I don't stow alcohol. They drank nothing
but mixers all the way to Mexico."

Amelia chuckled. "That sounds awful." Suni
checked the sails. Amelia sipped her drink, watching
her work. "How long have you been sailing?"

"All my life. I was born in Thailand. My mother
still lives in Bangkok. When I was six, she sent me
to stay with cousins, on the gulf. I worked on fishing
boats until I was twelve."

"What then?" Amelia pulled a micro-recorder from
her pocket.

"I ran away to be with my mother. She let me
live with her until I was fifteen, then she sent me to

the States." Suni sat beside her. "Are you sure you want the boring details?"

"Let me worry about what's boring. Do you like living here?"

"I didn't at first. I lived with more cousins, in San Diego, and I worked every summer on the docks. That was the good part, being around boats." She adjusted her visor. "I lied about how much money I made, and I traded work for gear every chance I got. I used to sail to the Catalina Islands. When I couldn't see the city, I pretended I was on the gulf, back in Thailand."

The recorder whirred. "Are you still homesick?"

"I'm never homesick when I'm sailing."

"Tell me about High Tide Adventures."

"I was supposed to use my college degree. That's why my cousins put up with me for so long, so I could pay them back. But I never got used to the business world. On the water, it's different. That's part of the attraction." Her smile was contagious. "People find it easy to relax on a boat. I bought *Little Bengal* two years ago."

"Your cousins must be pleased to have an entrepreneur in the family."

Her smile waned. "I don't see them. I'd really like to go back to Thailand to see my mother. I'm twenty-four. I haven't been home in nine years. Have you ever been to Thailand?"

"My magazine is exclusively domestic. When I was free-lancing, I saw Europe and the Costa Rican jungle. I've never been to Asia."

"Southeast Asia. There's a lot of Chinese influence, though, especially in Bangkok. Some of the old neighborhoods still have spirit houses. They're built on stilts like elaborate doll houses, with gilt and colored glass. They're supposed to bring protection and good luck. My mother thinks she has a bad spirit living with her. She won't let me be with her because she doesn't want her spirit to find me."

"She's serious?"

"It's useless to argue with superstition." She crushed her lemonade carton. "I left Thailand and became an American. But when I'm sailing, I don't feel like I have to be one nationality or the other. I can just be myself. What about you? Are you close to your family?"

"I was an only child. My parents could never understand why I turned out so warped. 'Devil's spawn,' 'bad seed,' those were my teenage nicknames. I ran away about once a month. I finally figured out I didn't have to go back. No sailboats, but I had a bicycle."

"When did you start writing?"

"In college. That reminds me, this is supposed to be my interview."

"If you print half of what I told you, no one will read it."

"Give me something better to write about," Amelia challenged.

"Sailing. Now get your butt over here and pull your weight."

They docked at sunset. Amelia wanted to roll out her sleeping bag and fall asleep.

Suni motioned for her to sit at the navigator's station. "You did pretty good for your first time out. How do you feel?"

"Like dead weight, since you ask."

Suni nodded. "Practice is over. When we set sail in the morning, you're my crew. Let's take a look at the charts."

She showed her the compass rose, pointing out meridians and parallels and explaining the conversion of degrees to nautical miles. Amelia looked at the tiny markings indicating buoy positions. They seemed to float, bobbing up and down on the map.

Suni put a hand between her shoulders. It moved to the back of her neck and squeezed. "Okay, sailor. Let's call it a day."

She sat back gratefully. "Do you work all your recruits this hard?"

"You're twice as good. I worked you twice as hard."

"Gee, thanks."

"I have a tradition. I never eat dinner on board the night before a voyage. Get washed up and I'll take you out."

Amelia stretched. "That's the best offer I've had all day. Besides lemonade." Lunch had been peanut butter and instant soup. "I'll eat anything but steak."

Suni laughed. "That's just as well. You'd better get used to seafood."

Chapter 9

The bar on Columbus Avenue looked like an empty set, waiting for stage props like full ashtrays and wet glasses. It took a moment for June's eyes to adjust to the dim interior. She glanced at her watch. Seven o'clock. Only a few women sat at the bar. At the pool table, a lone player was slapping practice shots.

The bartender took her time coming over. Her hair was stiff, spiky red, and she studied June's ID with sullen eyes. "Feds gone gay or what?" She wore a stud in her nose and a ring in her eyebrow.

"I'd like to ask you some questions about a rape and a murder that took place across the street, about two months ago. Do you remember?"

The bristling hair quivered a negative. She took in June's work clothes. "You're out of date, babe. Don't waste my time." She began to turn away.

June asked softly, "Who's your boss?" She received a shrug. June pointed to the phone behind the bar. "You might want to call her first. Just a suggestion. Then I'll call BATF. That stands for Bureau of Alcohol, Tobacco and Firearms." She surveyed the room. "If you'd like, I'll notify your patrons that you're closed for inventory. These things take time."

"I wasn't here."

"Who was?"

"Dee. Come back tomorrow. After eight."

"Okay. I'll be here tomorrow night. And Spiky?" She waited until angry eyes flashed up. "I appreciate your cooperation."

She threw the Porsche into gear and made a pass by the bar, just in case Spiky was curious. She hit the brakes as a light changed, ashamed of her tactics. She didn't have any BATF contacts, and no one was going to shut down a minor bar in a stale investigation. She had to loosen her grip on the steering wheel to change gears. Just thinking about the bar scene put her in a bad mood.

The club where she'd met Charlene had featured original art and a parquet floor. And a tea room in back. She reached for Elvis Costello and turned up the volume. It reminded her of Bass. She swerved into a parking spot and began pulling apart her car phone. Nothing. She felt carefully under the dash while her armpits got damp. If she got any more paranoid, she'd be the one about to jump from a bridge, and another agent would be talking her down. She eased back into traffic and rolled down her window.

Gretchen's drive was barely wide enough for one car. In her heyday, Gretchen had arrived at concerts by limousine. June pulled in and sat in the Porsche, listening to the stereo. Shane wanted her to share case notes with Al. She wondered if Shane knew that Al was from headquarters, possibly working for Colt. Every time she saw Al Rahman, he had a pencil behind his ear. He worked with hard copy. She'd never even seen him log on a computer. She shook her head. She didn't know what Al was after.

Costello started singing "Sneaky Feelings." She shut off the music. Tomorrow she'd do the bar interviews and close out the Wright investigation. She wondered if Amelia was wearing enough sun block in San Diego.

Amelia watched the sails, white and full, scudding through the air like clouds. Last night, sharing the cozy cabin with Suni had been more comfortable than she'd expected. They were respectful of each other without being modest, neither one making chit-chat to fill the silences. After dinner they'd gone quietly to bed, each to her own berth, like old roommates. When they got underway in the morning, they were already working like a team.

Now, in the mid-afternoon, Suni emerged from the hatchway, carrying juice boxes. Amelia smiled, enjoying the bronze glaze of her arms, the lemonade's refreshing cold.

Suni surveyed the water. "We're right on course."

"How can you tell?"

"While you've been admiring the wind in your sails, I've been plotting our position. You'll learn how before this voyage is over."

"You're all work and no play."

"Oh yeah? Do you think you could sail this boat by yourself?"

"I wouldn't want to."

"Too bad." She was still holding her juice box when she jumped overboard.

"Suni!" Amelia twisted, trying to hold the sails and tiller, frantically searching the water. A dark head bobbed in the swells. "Suni. Oh shit." She chucked her drink over the side. She tacked and eased off, slacking the sheets. "Suni, God damn you." She finally jibed, coming downwind. The bobbing figure waved and took a sip of lemonade.

"Harden up," Suni yelled.

Automatically, she shortened the mainsail. She overcompensated, and the sailboat heeled. Easing off again, she pushed the tiller, forcing the bow into the wind. She released the sails, letting them luff. Heading into the wind, she was still approaching too fast.

"Back the main," Suni called as the boat shot past.

She pushed the boom out, and the sailboat finally drifted to a stop. Belatedly, she threw the life ring, chagrined as Suni laughed.

"Not bad." Suni handed over her juice box and

levered herself on board. "Next time you're sailing close-hauled, jibe around to come downwind. It's faster. Not bad, though. You looked like a sailor."

"You did that on purpose."

"Yeah. Can I have my lemonade back, please?"

"Not a chance." Amelia brought the carton to her lips, feeling her hand shake.

She flushed as Suni laughed again. "See if you can get us back on course. I'm going below to change."

Amelia settled the boat on a beam reach. When the telltales were streaming evenly, she cleated the sails and lashed the tiller. Then she went below.

Suni emerged from the head wearing nothing but bikini bottoms. "Did I scare you?"

"I handled it."

"Yes, you did. Very well, too."

"Is that a standard part of the training?"

"Not for everyone. I've had crews that would've left me behind." She toweled her hair, still naked except for the bikini briefs.

Amelia looked at her compact breasts. There were no tan lines. She dropped her eyes. Suni's stomach muscles were hard and flat. "Are you going to get dressed?"

"I'm going topside to warm up."

On deck, Suni lay on her back, using a life jacket to cushion her head. Amelia picked up a coil of rope, her fingers automatically tying knots. Suni's breathing had slowed; water droplets glistened on her chest. Eyes closed, she rubbed lotion into her skin, then stretched. Amelia bent over her.

An eye cracked open. "You're blocking the sun."

"You missed a spot." She rubbed lotion into her shoulder.

"Thanks."

"Don't mention it." She slipped the rope over Suni's wrists. Both eyes flashed open. "Wouldn't want to lose you again." She pulled hard, tightening the rope. Suni's chest rose. The tempo of her breathing increased. "Are you scared?"

"I'm not scared of you, Amelia. But I can't stand half-done chores. Can you finish what you've started?"

Amelia straddled her. "Are we on course?"

Suni squinted. "I can't tell from my current position." The private smile was back. "I guess you're in charge." She brought her arms down, hands bound in front of her, reaching for Amelia.

She tugged Suni's arms up. "Don't touch me yet." She unbuttoned her blouse. Underneath, her bra felt tight. She peeled it off. Sun spread like oil on her back. She rocked forward, rubbing slowly, letting their breasts connect, then their lips. She sank her hands into sun-dappled hair. When she raised up, her nipple was inches from Suni's mouth.

"Amelia, please." Her breast tightened, tingled from the whispered breath. "Let me touch you."

"I'll touch you first." The bikini slipped away, and more dark hair curled in her palm. She stroked lightly. Her lips touched a nipple. She bit gently; then she was stroking deeply and sucking hard.

Suni's body rippled beneath her. "Amelia. Please."

No longer pretending to be in control, she drew the ropes from Suni's wrists. Unbound, the hands stripped her shorts off and pushed her down. She couldn't breathe. It didn't matter. Mouth on Suni, she swallowed her breath. Chests connected, her ribs expanded. Her blood pulsed and air, air was everywhere — sweeping her body, driving the boat. She drank kisses like water and her tongue licked salt. She arched when she came, and her eyes opened. Overhead, she saw nothing but sails.

They docked at sunset and walked together through a sandy marketplace. Faces seemed warmer as the sun dipped lower. Everywhere she looked, Amelia saw brown skin and black hair. She was too white; as white as the teeth that chattered and bickered. She wanted to absorb color from bunches of fruit, buckets of fish, even mongrel dogs and dirt. The fiery sun hovered and the ocean turned orange; heat was swallowed by a turquoise sea. She linked her arm through Suni's, ignoring the hooted taunts of men, envying the women their laughing banter.

Suni bought fruit, and something called *pulpo*. On the beach, she set up a grill. Amelia slipped her toes into the cooling sand. The air smelled like seaweed and smoke.

"I didn't know you spoke Spanish."

Suni rubbed hot sauce on the fish. "Enough to get by."

"Do you still speak Thai?"

"It's been a while. I don't get much chance to practice."

"You could have been a linguist." She opened bottles of beer, gave one to Suni.

"I thought about it. I picked up English pretty fast. But then I discovered computers. I majored in computer science."

"I thought you said business."

"I said I didn't like the business world. I loved computers, though. I was lucky; I never expected to go to college. But I survived all the crap my cousins dished out by being competitive. When the oldest one signed up for the SATs, I did too, and I got a perfect math score. We both got scholarships, but mine was better."

Amelia laughed. "I'm sailing with a rogue genius."

"Everything has drawbacks." Suni cut into a piece of fruit. "Here, try some papaya."

It was succulent, pinkish-orange, the center full of round black seeds. Amelia bit into the ripe flesh and licked the juice. It tasted like melon and honey. "What's the seafood selection tonight?"

"Octopus."

"You're joking."

"It's a delicacy. These are young and tender." Amelia stared morosely at the grill. "Cheer up." Suni's voice was warm, like the glowing coals. "You're going to love it. I promise."

Suni had been right about the octopus. Tangy and hot, it had burned her lips, and she'd chased the spice with icy beer. She couldn't remember when food had tasted so good. Lying in the double berth, Amelia reached for her, stroked a hand along her flank. Wrapping her from behind, she cupped a breast and flicked the nipple. Suni rolled, then moved on top, searching Amelia's body with her hands, then her mouth.

The boat pulled at its mooring; ropes sighed, eased and strained. Amelia grazed the nipple with her teeth; her fingers teased folds of skin. Suni softened. In her mind, Amelia pushed not just fingers but her whole body between the spreading legs. She took her hand away, replaced it with her mouth. She drank the opening, salty and sweet as fruit from the blue Pacific.

They spent the next day lounging on the beach and making love on deck. When they set sail for San Diego, Suni took command of the boat, moving gracefully. Land receded. Amelia made fast the sheets and held the tiller, resting her arm around Suni's waist. They sailed past sunset, and Amelia imagined that the water was a velvet cloak, the breeze a fluttering scarf. And the stars were a broken necklace tumbled on dark breasts.

June reached into the depths of her closet for her tightest jeans. She'd worn them to the D.C. nightclub where she'd met Charlene, when she'd been trying to get a life with more than guns and memories. For six years, the guns had stayed locked in a safe, but the nightmares had followed her to and from work like car-pooling ghouls.

She pulled on the jeans. They were still tight. She peeled them off and stepped back into her pleated trousers. The tailored pants made her look conservative. She unclipped her beeper. Better. She tossed it in her underwear drawer. For parties, Charlene had worn slinky dresses or clingy skirts. An image of Amelia came to mind — baggy shorts and a neon windbreaker. She slipped out of her jacket and shoulder harness, unbuttoned her blouse. With a demure band of lace, even her bra was traditional.

Frustrated and half-dressed, she faced herself in the mirror. She'd always been too tall, too bulky. What kind of body had Charlene really wanted? Who had she gone to when she hadn't wanted June? Someone smaller, lighter, more petite. Someone like Amelia? Instinctively, she knew Charlene would have hated Amelia. The thought made her smile at her reflection.

She rummaged in her dresser for a polo shirt, resigned to look sporty. She tripped over the jeans, still on the floor. Scooping them up, she carried them into the kitchen, poking through the utility drawer for a scissors. When the expensive denim had been reduced to rags, she felt ready for a night at the bar.

She parked three blocks away and walked past the subway stop. There was a Chinese restaurant on the corner. Garbage sacks and crates of broccoli stalks were piled near a dumpster. She slowed as she approached the bank. Through a crack in the blinds, she glimpsed blotters and pen sets, dust covers over computers. The side door was sealed and padlocked, the cement still damp from a recent rain.

It had rained that night. She knew because the police report had made note of Amelia's clothes, soaked through. As she entered the alley, she accidentally scuffed the toe of one of her loafers. She could barely make out the colors — a streak of tan from her scarred shoe, and muddy gray cement.

Halfway in, she touched the wall. It gave away nothing — no visual imprint or hint of emotion. Involuntarily, she made a fist. She surveyed the pitted ground, the puddles, the garbage. Then she crossed the street, heading for the bar.

The bartender nearest the door could have been a model, her blond hair darkened by shadows and sexy highlights. A second bartender worked the far end. At eight-thirty, the tables were filling up. On the dance floor, couples were loose, giving each other room to move. June took a stool.

"Get you something?"

The husky voice made her look again. Transgendered. She'd almost been attracted. "Tonic." When the drink arrived, she put down a bill and opened her ID. "Take a break." She moved to a table. The bartender brought change, carrying a coffee mug. Behind the bar, a glass broke and someone swore. June saw a broom and recognized the bristling hair. "I don't think Spiky likes me."

"She's jealous." Trim hips swiveled into a chair. "She goes for macho women. So do I." Her mouth parted in a dazzling, lipsticked smile. She crossed long, denim-covered legs. A flowing blouse covered her crotch. "Honey, I don't have all night. You wanted to talk?"

June concentrated on perfectly made-up eyes. "Do you know Amelia Wright?"

"She's a regular celebrity, popular enough for a fan club if she'd just pay attention. And I'm not talking about press releases and signed photos. It's kind of sweet the way the baby-faced butches are always crushed out. But she doesn't encourage it.

118

She's funny that way, almost shy. Maybe she'll see more action now that she's dumped that ball-and-chain girlfriend."

June squeezed lime into her drink. Poor Bryanna. She made such a bad impression. "When was the last time you saw Amelia?"

"She hasn't been back since the rape." Red lips compressed. "All men should take my example."

"Was anyone with her that night?"

"Who else? The girlfriend." Her mouth puckered like she'd tasted something sour. "Bryanna, I think that's her name. She's been around a few times since, by herself. Last time, she was putting the moves on some stupid college kid. I carded the kid and threw her out, for her own protection."

"On the night of the rape, you saw Amelia and Bryanna together?"

"Saw them, served them, heard them argue."

"What did you hear?"

"It sounded like a classic break-up scene to me. They didn't stay long." She frowned. "I must've been in the back because I didn't see them leave. The next thing I know, the girls are screaming for an ambulance."

June leaned forward. "Who, exactly, did the screaming?"

The bartender ran a polished finger around the lip of her mug. "Did you ever play a party game called 'Operator'? One person starts a message and passes it on, and it gets passed around the room. The person at the end of the line has to repeat it back, but by that time, it's so garbled it's embarrassing." Glossy lips sipped coffee. "I made the phone call, but don't ask me who sent the message. Between you, me and my heart of hearts, I always thought the girlfriend was the Good Sam shooter."

June studied the high forehead, hazel eyes and sculpted cheekbones. "Why do you think it was Bryanna?"

"One night she was sitting at the bar, crying into her Margarita. I deplore mopey customers. Anyhow, she has a gun. It stands to reason she's Good Sam."

"Do you know for certain that Bryanna Waters is in possession of a handgun?"

The bartender gave a husky laugh. "You cops. You always sound the same." She patted June's hand. "Honey, of course I'm sure. Between the tequila and the tears, she told me so herself."

She called Shane at home. "Waters probably lied about owning a handgun. I've checked the listing and I know she doesn't have a license. Can you get me a warrant? I'd like to have a little chat with her about the Commonwealth's gun laws."

"I'll call you back."

She drove to the Jamaica Plain neighborhood. At Bryanna's house, a bedroom light was on. By ten-thirty, it winked out. It was eleven-thirty when Shane called her car phone.

"The window of opportunity closed two months ago. You're going to need more than the bartender's say-so."

"That first investigation ended before most of the women were interviewed. The local force thought they were looking for a man. Isn't a change in the suspect's gender a good enough reason to open this up?"

"It's not specific evidence against Waters." She could almost hear him smile. "Gender's only useful if you want to ask her out."

"Thanks. I'll keep that in mind."

"Do you really think Waters is Good Sam?"

"I don't care if she's the Holy Virgin incarnate. If she's got an illegal weapon, I want to find it and have her prosecuted through the local authorities."

"You're just pissed because she lied to you. The only way you're going to get a warrant is if you have evidence linking Waters directly to the robbery or kidnapping. Or find someone who saw her in the alley. The night is young," he teased. "I'll bet there are plenty of good-looking women who want to talk to you." When she was silent, he said, "Colt wants an update."

"I'm at the Waters' address. I'm going to wake her up."

"Remember to knock politely."

She banged on the door until wind chimes rattled and lights came on next door. A sleepy-eyed waif with a puffy, adolescent face finally answered.

"Hi." She held up her wallet. "I'm a federal agent. May I come in?" The girl took an involuntary step back. June sent the door crashing. "Where is she?" She was standing in a tiny living room. Light spilled over carpeted stairs. She took them three at a time, following the smell of incense. Sheets were thrown back on an empty bed. Over her shoulder, she heard an unmistakable metallic click as someone cocked a revolver.

She turned slowly. The girl no longer looked

sleepy. She stood with both arms stiffly extended, trembling behind the twenty-two caliber handgun. Good Sam had used a thirty-eight. June wondered fleetingly if Bryanna was hiding with the murder weapon in the bathroom.

She said icily, "I thought Bryanna didn't believe in guns."

"Who . . . Who are you?" The revolver shook.

"You're holding it too tight."

"Huh?"

"The gun. You're shaking too much and holding it too tightly. You've never held a handgun before, have you?"

"No." The chin quivered.

Great, another crier. What was it with Bryanna and tears? "Is that Bryanna's gun?" The head nodded. "Then put it down. It doesn't belong to you."

The girl looked doubtfully at the revolver, then seemed to remember why she was holding it. Her shoulders stiffened. "Who are you?"

She lapsed into a patient tone. "My name is June Gavin. I work for the FBI. Would you like to see my identification again?" She received another nod. "Okay. My wallet is in my pocket. I don't want to scare you, so why don't you get it for me?" She slipped out of her jacket. Wide eyes stared at her shoulder holster. "That's my service weapon. I'm allowed to carry a gun. I don't think you are, though." Admonishment tinged her words. Guilt crept into the child-like eyes. "That's okay. I'll walk you through the procedure." She held up her jacket. "This pocket has my credentials. Check for the wallet, that's the first thing." Unsteady steps brought the girl closer. "You're doing fine. Now check the pocket."

The left hand reached out, and the right hand, unused to the weight of a gun, dipped. In one motion, June dropped the jacket and closed her fingers around the shaky wrist. The gun was so sweaty it slid without resistance into her hand. She uncocked the hammer and flipped open the chamber to check for cartridges. There were none.

"Well, well. Lots of intent and no ammunition. What a bad combination." She dropped the gun into her jacket pocket and held up her ID. "Take another look."

Guilty eyes focused on her badge. "Bryanna's not here." Her voice wavered.

Please, June thought, *don't let her cry.* She said firmly, "I'd like you to go downstairs and make some tea."

"Herbal tea?"

She grimaced. "Herbal it is. Go." She ushered the nightgown-clad figure out of the room, then pulled her gun and looked into closets, the bathroom and an empty study, limiting herself to a plain-view search. Now that a crime had been committed, if you could call sweating on an empty revolver criminal, she was welcome to keep the twenty-two. She holstered her Browning and trudged downstairs. The dining room and TV room turned up no thirty-eight caliber weapons, bank loot or ransom notes. Back in the kitchen, two tea cups smelled suspiciously like chamomile.

She helped herself to a chair. "Are you Bryanna's guest?"

"She asked me to stay."

"Where is she?"

"On retreat."

"I see. And where is that?"

"The women's retreat. In the mountains."

She sipped tea and scalded her tongue. "Do you know which mountains?"

"Oh . . . I think . . . New Hampshire."

"And you're keeping an eye on things while she's away?"

"Bryanna's done so much for me. When she asked, I couldn't say no."

"Did she give you the gun as a safety precaution? For protection?" Shoulders slumped guiltily. "What's your name?"

"Mabel."

"How old are you, Mabel?"

Her voice was soft. "Nineteen."

"How did you meet Bryanna?"

"I get college credit for volunteering at the women's health center. Bryanna came and gave a lecture. She has so much information to give, but she's a good listener, too."

"It's nice of you to look after her house. I guess you got cold during the night and needed an extra pair of socks. So you were searching through the sock drawer and you found the gun. Is that what happened?"

Mabel hunched over her tea. "I was hungry."

"You found the gun in the cookie jar?"

"It said biscotti."

June sighed. "Finish your tea. I'll fix us a snack."

Bryanna's cupboard held Swedish licorice, Swiss chocolate and several brands of Italian cookies. And she had a freezer full of ice cream. A rattling Ben &

Jerry's container produced an assortment of cold bullets.

"Okay, Mabel. It's time for bed."

"You're staying?" Wide eyes looked hopeful.

She suppressed a shudder. "I'm leaving now. You can go back to bed." She said more gently, "I'm sorry I woke you." The girl headed obligingly for the stairs. "Mabel? Did Bryanna leave a number where she can be reached? In case of an emergency?"

Mabel padded to the phone table. "She left a brochure. The mountains sound so spiritual."

June shoved the brochure in her pocket and grabbed her keys. Colt would get his report, but not tonight. Not after the bar scene, Mabel and Sleepytime tea.

"Gretchen," she prayed as she started the Porsche, "please be awake and please bring the vodka."

Suni kissed Amelia chastely, on the cheek. "You'd better write one hell of a story."

"It'll be an abbreviated version. My editor pays for sports, not sex."

"So narrow-minded."

Amelia smiled. "I'm sorry to be back on land. I could have kept sailing forever."

"Don't you know the world is round? You'd get bored going around in circles."

"Do you ever wish you could escape, sail away and never come back?"

Suni said seriously, "Sometimes I think losing

myself in the ocean would be the best thing I could do."

"You'd leave a lot of unhappy customers behind. If I have anything to say about it, and I do, you're going to be very busy."

"True enough. Good-bye Amelia. I'm glad we met."

Chapter 10

Amelia slammed open the cottage door, dropped her duffel and grabbed the ringing phone. "Hello." The camera bag banged her hip.

"Amelia? I've been trying to reach you all weekend."

She heard the plaintive tone in Bryanna's voice and cursed the technology of her long-distance service. It was late Sunday night. "I was on assignment."

"You're gone so much."

"It's my job." She wanted to hang up, or hurl the

cordless phone through a window. She wanted to do anything but explain herself to Bryanna. She said curtly, "It helps. I feel better when I'm working."

"Oh, baby, I know. You're trying so hard. I just wish you'd let me be there for you." There was a pause. "I called to wish you a happy birthday. You're thirty-three tomorrow. I didn't want you to think I'd forgotten. I was hoping . . . well, I thought maybe I could help you celebrate."

"I just got in and I'm really tired."

"I'm sorry. I shouldn't push."

The phone call followed the usual obstacle course of guilt, pressure, apology. Bryanna didn't get it that the relationship was over. Eventually, she'd have to tell her again. But she'd tried to say it once. And ended up in a putrid alley, her nose broken, blood and bile trapped in her throat.

His breath was clammy. She could feel him, coarse and hairy as he forced himself in. He crushed her, grunting rhythmically. He'd yanked her pants down; now he pushed a hand up her shirt. He still wore his gloves, and for that she was grateful. The leather felt impersonal, infinitely better than skin. He squeezed so hard the pain made her arch involuntarily. He slapped her down. Water had puddled on the ground and it seeped under her jacket. Her back was raw and cold; her face and head felt feverishly hot. She swallowed blood. Briefly, before her throat filled again, she smelled garbage, the rank aroma of rotten vegetables. Her mind seized the thought and wouldn't let it go. The vegetables made sense. Finally, she remembered — on the corner, there was a Chinese restaurant. She imagined she smelled stir-fry. Her mouth and nose were full of blood. She choked, turned her head and spat. She stared at the wall.

His weight disappeared so suddenly that she gasped. A fit of coughing gripped her and she rolled on her side. Pain lanced her chest. She heard the crack a second after she saw his boot. It was as though his foot was disconnected from his body, as though this moment of pain was separate, severed from other experience. She wasn't yet aware of ripped tissue between her legs, of ruptured blood vessels beneath her swollen eyes. She was blessedly numb, watching his foot hurtle toward her. She'd thought the gunshot was the sound of splintering ribs.

She heard a thud. She stared at the floor before she realized she'd dropped the camera bag.

"Amelia? Amelia!"

"I'm . . . okay." Air seemed a long way off. "I went sailing." She spoke dully, trying to visualize the sloop. She focused on the sails. All she had to do was keep them full.

Bryanna was babbling about camping. "Well, it's not camping, exactly. We have cabins, and cushy bunks. Don't you remember that trip we always wanted to take? You remember," she insisted. "The women's mountain retreat. Well, I'm here and it's beautiful. I thought it would be a nice birthday treat for you to get away. You'll love it, Amelia, I know you will. Please come?"

She opened her mouth to say no but saliva had dried to chalk.

"I thought you could write an article," Bryanna suggested. "There's rock climbing."

She closed her eyes. In her mind, boulders grew into cliffs, stretching skyward. As she climbed, panic crumbled like pebbles and fell away. Under her palms, there was hard-edged, unfeeling granite. The closer she got to the stone, the less her emotions mattered.

She opened her eyes. "I'll come."

"You will?" Bryanna sounded surprised. "Oh, baby, that's wonderful. Come tomorrow, on Monday. We'll have the whole week together."

"I need to do laundry. I'll come on Tuesday."

"I'm at Sunset Ridge Retreat in the White Mountains. Get a pencil and I'll give you directions."

Amelia scribbled the information. *I never loved you. I thought I needed you. I'm sorry I used you.* One thought flared into another, like lips blowing a spark. Anger simmered. Bryanna had used her, too. She'd consumed her, closed around her the way a caterpillar spins a cocoon. But no Monarch had emerged. When the suffocating husk had broken open, the relationship was empty. She hung up the phone and sank to the floor, hugging her knees. She'd taken every decay-tinged offering, afraid to refuse, believing she'd starve. Looking down at herself, she almost laughed. She was starving anyway.

Sure, Bryanna. I'll come to the mountains. I'm going to make sure you know it's over. I'll go

climbing, and when I get back, I'm going to change
my phone number.

It was too much effort to unpack or go to bed.
She crawled into her sleeping bag. On Monday
morning, she called Marj.

Her disbelief boomed. "You want to go on a god-
damn retreat?" Work was going well, Amelia
surmised. Marj only swore on good days. As budgets
grew tight and deadlines approached, she snapped out
orders in terse, unembellished prose. Profanity was a
positive mood indicator. "And why on God's green
earth should I send you to a women's retreat? In
New Hampshire, of all places."

"I'm going rock climbing. The retreat is a new
angle. Sort of like cliff-hanger goes New Age."

"New Age is dying," Marj grumbled, "but not fast
enough."

"Half of our readership is queer. Think of this
story as a vertical view of the Michigan women's
festival."

"Twenty-six point four percent of our readers
identify as lesbian or bisexual. Don't exaggerate the
market. Furthermore, Michigan is a household word.
Who can find New Hampshire on the map?"

"Since when do we tell anyone to take the beaten
path?"

"Shit. Good point."

"I'll be gone two days, three max."

"Take film. I don't have to remind you that solo
climbing is extremely dangerous."

"Thanks, Marj. You're gonna love this one."

"You owe me two. Sailboats and rocks. And I sure as hell better not hear that you've been meditating."

" 'Bye, Marj."

"One more thing, sweetie." Amelia tensed. She preferred profanity to Marj's endearments. "It hasn't escaped our notice that it's your birthday. BJ's giving you a surprise party."

"No way. Talk him out of it."

"I tried. He did your horoscope or something. He thinks it's time for you to meet someone."

"That's ridiculous, even for BJ."

"He has the best intentions."

"Okay. He can have a party tomorrow. I'll be gone."

"He knows you're in town. He's coming up tonight with some friends."

"Marj —"

"And cake and ice cream. Did I mention that?"

"BJ's bringing sugar?"

"I do have some power of persuasion. Listen to me, Amelia. The way you get through this — and you know what I'm talking about — is your business. But you still have friends who care about you. Give BJ a break. Let him have his party. And if you can't be grateful, at least act surprised."

"Thanks for the warning."

"By the way, Lady Hercules is looking for you."

"I can't deal with this." She threw the phone on the couch and her body after it, then sat up and surveyed the cottage. Her half-unpacked duffel littered the floor. Damp clothes had dried, draped over her bicycle. Camera, sunglasses and tape recorder cluttered the coffee table. She should probably roll the sleeping bag. She lay back. Fuck the cleaning. If her guests didn't like her personal space, too bad. She reached under the couch for a climbing rope and shaped a noose. "Bring anything but chocolate, BJ, and you're a dead man."

The party felt like it was happening under water. She swam through the small crowd, handing out dishes of ice cream. She pretended to chat and smiled until her face felt like cardboard. When everyone had cake and ice cream, she trailed after BJ, afraid to leave his side. Time was jagged. People spoke but it took them forever to finish a sentence. Music sounded far off. Candles and party streamers melted together like a collage.

BJ sat beside her, sipping ginseng. During a break in the music she said too loudly, "This isn't fun." Her subdued guests began a hasty clean-up. She tugged on his sleeve. "Get them out of here."

He looked at her closely. "It's hard to leave you alone like this."

"You haven't seen the worst of it."

"That's my point. Someone should."

"Not you." She indicated the awkward friends. "Not them."

He sighed. "What about the mess?"

"Just go."

He ushered everyone outside and turned back. "You can't isolate yourself forever."

She said to the closed door, "Watch me."

* * * * *

The porch light was on as June climbed the cottage steps. She knocked once, then took a half-step back as the door was yanked open.

"What'd you forget?" Amelia stared. "Oh. What are you doing here?"

"Who were you expecting?"

"BJ. He just left."

"May I come in?"

"Do I have a choice?" She stomped across the room.

"This would be easier if we were both polite." June stepped inside. Party streamers fell from the ceiling, twisting colorfully around the kayak and mountain bike. A flock of balloons hovered in a corner, migrating to a deflated finale. "Sorry I missed the party. Happy birthday."

"My former friends decided to resurrect my social life. They should've left it dead and buried."

June walked into the kitchen. A half-eaten cake lay collapsed on the counter, sprawled between soggy ice cream cartons. Bowls and plates straggled toward the trash.

"Your guests should have stayed for clean-up."

"I kicked them out. You're next."

June took off her jacket and rolled her sleeves. She'd left the Browning locked in the Porsche. "Give me ten minutes." She shooed Amelia from the kitchen, then cleared and sponged the counters. She found clean trash bags and called, "Do you want to save the cake?" When there was no answer, she dumped the sodden mess into the trash. She located garbage cans through a back door and hefted the sacks outside. When the dishes were stacked to dry, she walked back into the living room. Amelia was on

134

the couch, her eyes open and unfocused, limbs and muscles twitching.

June sat down carefully. "Amelia." Her legs and arms jerked. "Amelia, it's June. I'm sitting next to you." Amelia's whole body spasmed. She gasped, and her eyes squeezed shut. "Don't fight it," June said softly. "It'll pass." Amelia shuddered. "The air comes back," June said. Slowly, Amelia's clenched hands loosened. With a sob, she dropped her head. June waited. Amelia cried, harsh, choked grief. When the tears fell silently, June said, "I'll hold you." Amelia didn't struggle. June soothed a hand through tangled curls. "How often do you have flashbacks?"

"Not on the boat." She said raggedly, "It was better on the boat. God, I can't stand crying."

"Sometimes it helps."

She sat up. "Rafting, sailing, climbing. Anything's better than crying." She wiped away tears. "My chest gets so tight I can't breathe, like all the air is pushed out. I need to move."

"What you're going through is normal."

Amelia glared. "How the hell do you know? Oh, I forgot ─── you're Killer-Agent Gavin. You know everything."

"No, I don't."

June couldn't comprehend why she had her father's memories. They were his nightmares and belonged in his head, not hers. She saw faces from old photos. While she watched, their expressions contorted; their bodies crumpled or exploded. One by one they stood before her and died, an endless line of carnage.

Sometimes they called her father's name. *"Hey, Bud. Don't leave us to die."*

"You're already dead," she assured them. *"I can't get you all out. Some of you are going to burn."*

She said, "I really don't know what you're going through, Amelia. Do you have any of BJ's beer?"

"In the fridge. He brought a fresh batch tonight."

"What can I get for you? Tea?"

"Stop it. Stop trying to take care of me. I don't need —"

"You don't need anything," June snapped. "I know the drill."

Amelia flung back, "You weren't invited. I don't want your help."

"Fine," June said coldly. "We'll just pick up where we left off. Before human pain interrupted." She stalked into the kitchen and yanked open the refrigerator. Beer bottle in hand, she began a methodic search of drawers, pulling them open and shoving them closed.

"What are you looking for?" Amelia had followed her into the kitchen.

"Bottle opener."

"Here." The utensil lay harmlessly on the counter.

"Thank you." She applied too much force and sent the cap skidding across the floor.

Amelia said, "I'll make some tea."

"Fine." She strode back to the living room and sat on the couch, one foot tapping. Amelia came out of the kitchen. June crossed her legs to still her foot. "How was San Diego?"

"Great sailing." Amelia sipped from a steaming mug. "I don't want to make small talk. Why are you here?"

"I found out that your ex-girlfriend has a gun."

"No way. Bryanna wouldn't go near a gun."

"Do you eat biscotti?"

"Those dry Italian cookies? Yuk."

"How about French vanilla ice cream?"

"No, thanks. If you're planning a party, please don't invite me."

"I saw a revolver and ammunition at Bryanna's house."

Amelia set down her mug. "Bryanna's out of town. When were you in her house?"

"Have you been in contact with her?"

"Yes, as a matter of fact. She called yesterday. I'm going to the White Mountains to break up with her again and do some rock climbing."

"I'd prefer that you didn't see her right now."

"Why? Do you still think she shot my rapist?"

"The gun I recovered is the wrong caliber. She might have another one."

"You're unbelievable. Take your action-figure fantasies somewhere else. I'm going climbing. Don't try to stop me."

June stood up. "Be careful, Amelia."

"Fuck you."

She took her half-finished drink to the kitchen and poured it down the drain. Determined strides carried her to the door.

"Don't go."

She turned. Amelia's lips were pressed together but the words had already escaped.

She said, "I can stay for a while."

Amelia stood up. "I need a bath."

* * * * *

137

Amelia shut the bathroom door. Alone, she undressed and washed. Wearing a towel, she made her way to the bedroom. The bedcovers had been turned down and the bedside lamp was on. June was standing by the dresser. In the soft light, she looked distant, calm. Amelia sat on the edge of the bed.

June said, "I'll be in the living room."

"Don't go." She heard them again, those two weak words.

June was watching her. "Are you afraid you'll have another flashback?"

"No. Not now."

"How can I help?" Her tone was so professional.

"Why don't you take a shower."

June hesitated. "Sure. I'll get a few things from my car."

The front door opened. A moment later, she heard June come back in, and the scrape of metal as the latch was secured. Amelia waited until she heard the shower, then let the towel drop. Naked, she slipped between the sheets. She thought of Suni — small, sun-warmed curves. She remembered blue-green water, brown skin and the taste of salt. Always, the taste of salt. Gradually, her thoughts stilled. The mattress dipped. June, large and solid in faded sweats, wet hair combed behind each ear, sat beside her.

June's hand traced the bedding, touched her. "I shouldn't be here like this, Amelia. If you're feeling safe, then I'll go."

Amelia watched the rise and fall of her chest. She reached for June's shoulders, grasped the sweatshirt and began to pull.

June caught her hand. "You'll be furious if I let this happen."

"I know. And I'll be angry if you make me stop. You can't win, Agent Gavin. You'd better find a way to deal with the situation."

"I'll deal."

June's arms raised as Amelia tugged the sweatshirt over her head. Unlike her own muscles, carved under the skin even at rest, June's strength lacked definition, until she moved. Pectorals contracted as she leaned on an arm. Amelia stared at the heavy breasts. She cupped one and placed her thumb on the nipple. She waited for her body to betray her, for lungs to strip themselves of air, limbs to spasm, skin to sweat. But her ribs rose smoothly. She turned on her side. June lifted her hand from her breast, but clasped it against her leg. Under the cotton sweatpants, her thigh was solid.

"Amelia?"

"I want you."

June's arm circled her. Amelia pushed the sweatpants past her hips. June kicked them off and slid under the covers. When she felt her full weight, Amelia gasped. June gazed down, serious, questioning, tender. Too tender. Amelia shut the light. Then she rocked against her, pummeling flesh even as June embraced her.

She made love to June with her whole body, biting, clawing, fingers digging. She batted away June's caresses and pulled her on top, clinging to her breasts and wrapping her legs around her thigh. She bit her shoulder. June held her tightly. Amelia pressed up into her, a furious repetition, feeling the strong arms loosen only when her spasms abated.

She closed her eyes. "Whatever you want."

June settled herself, spreading wetness. Startled, Amelia opened her eyes.

June smiled. "What did you expect?"

She felt soft kisses — first at the corners of her eyes, then on the lids. June moved slowly, kissing her lips — first the edges, then the center. She tasted June's tongue.

June drew her mouth away. "Now," she whispered. "Let's do it my way."

Tender kisses turned throaty and full. Amelia sank into the bed. The body that had absorbed her passion flowed over her. When she resisted, June stopped. Only her hands, warm and large, continued to stroke. When she lay still, the body caresses resumed — slow, whip-like undulations. Gradually, movement shortened until there was only one point of contact, one fulcrum balanced evenly, exactly between them. Then the connection disappeared.

She arched up but the touch was gone. June sat beside her, patient, waiting. She lay back. Then June's hands were on her hips; lips touched between her legs. She struggled and the mouth moved away. When she was quiet, the tongue returned, subtle, then insistent. Soft tissue swelled. Inside, emotion unraveled like twine. Then the sensation burst open. Physical weight crushed her but it was only June, holding her close.

June dreamed fire.

Carbon and hydrogen devoured oxygen; air disappeared with a sucking sound. Her father fought

140

the flames, eyes round in his grimy face, hands huge
on his axe. The axe turned into a gun. He stood, the
heat like a halo around him, and pointed the
axe-turned-gun straight at her heart.

He called, "Don't be afraid."

She crawled toward him but she was never in
time. Fire engulfed him and the gun exploded; his
skin became ribbons of flame. She tried to scream but
when she opened her mouth, fire roared out.

She coughed herself awake. She never knew what
would happen if she reached him. Would he shoot
her? Or should she take the gun and turn it on him
so that he could die with blood instead of fire in his
veins?

Beside her, Amelia was tossing fitfully. Carefully,
June tidied the covers, pulled her close.

"You owe me." Amelia's voice was husky,
stubborn.

"Mmm?"

"You never told me your story."

"Later." She closed her eyes but couldn't sleep.
She held Amelia, who was also pretending to rest.

"Hello, dear. Sleepless night? Or did you wake up
early?"

"Hi, Gretch. Come on in." June was in her
sweatsuit, the memory of Amelia's body still warming
her skin. The sun was coming up and she had the
kettle on. When it whistled, she filled the teapot.
"I'm sorry I didn't come home last night. Will you
join me for tea?"

"I wondered when you were going to stop

spending your nights with an ancient widow. And I'm not looking for sympathy," Gretchen scolded. "I'm prying. An accomplished spy like you should know the difference."

June held her mug to her lips and breathed in the aromatic steam. Her mind closed around an image of Amelia, legs wrapping her thigh, then her pelvis tilting. *Arrogance,* she accused herself. As though one night of sex could compensate for months of pain. As though tenderness could make up for brutality. She sipped her tea. They'd shared more than tenderness. At dawn, bending to kiss Amelia, she'd almost acknowledged it. But with her nightmare hanging like heat over the bed, she hadn't said anything.

"Whoever she is," Gretchen cooed, "let her get some sleep. Then give her a call."

June was at her desk early and got to work at the computer. Al hadn't come in yet. She checked her e-mail. Bass had left her a message. *The bridge is still up.* It was his way of telling her he didn't have answers.

"Damn it, Bass. If you're not careful, it's going to come down on both of our necks."

She opened a file and reviewed her notes. She'd been back at the bar on Friday night, interviewing patrons. Some of them remembered the night of Amelia's rape; no one remembered seeing Bryanna come back into the bar. No one knew who had tipped the bartender to call 911. Yesterday, she'd met with Shane and typed her notes. But she'd been reluctant to close the file. Last night she'd been with Amelia. Today, there was no excuse. Colt's query blinked on her screen. Her final report was due.

Amelia Wright's rapist had been shot and killed by a woman, Good Sam, still unidentified. Bryanna Waters had walked out of the bar with Amelia, then gone to the home of BJ Honda. No one that June had interviewed had seen Amelia or anyone else in the alley. No one at the bar could say if they'd seen the Good Sam shooter. If she'd been in their midst, there was no way to know. Colt's hope that Amelia would provide information leading to Good Sam hadn't been borne out.

Perhaps Good Sam knew who had kidnapped the bank vice president. Perhaps, as Colt suspected, Good Sam had done the bank robbery to taunt the kidnappers, and they'd retaliated. The kidnappers had maintained their silence. Colt couldn't negotiate for the vice president's release. Without Good Sam to help him locate the kidnappers, he had little chance of bringing the hostage home. But June couldn't find Good Sam. Amelia had been a dead end lead.

She finished the report and copied it to Shane and Colt. Before she turned off the computer, Al Rahman walked in. He peered over her shoulder.

"Anything interesting?"

She saved her document and closed the file. "Nothing but unsolved cases. How about you?"

He uncapped his thermos and poured himself a cup of coffee. "We should share notes. Maybe you're overlooking some details."

She glanced at her watch. It would be a good time to put in some practice at the shooting range. She said, "Sure, Al. Another time."

Chapter 11

Her world was granite. In every direction, textured rock extended from her hands and feet. Using fingers and toes, she dug in, finding the rough edges that held her as securely as rope. She wedged herself in a crevice. Rock scraped inside her thighs. She angled, reached up, found a protrusion and embraced it. She molded to the surface, absorbing direction. Where there had been no contour, a crack appeared; where she had found no toe-hold, suddenly a ledge. Below was hardness. Overhead, only glaring sun. She smelled chalk and grit layered on sweat. She became two-dimensional, one side solid, the other made of air. Muscle and sinew knotted together, hoisted her up. She climbed in a jagged line, ascending the cliff.

Two-thirds of the way up, she suspended her camera and activated the timer. Anchored by ropes, she rappelled part-way down, climbing again while the camera automatically focused and recorded her efforts. She made her way to the top. Even with a wide-angle lens, she had trouble taking in the view. BJ would have known instinctively — the best settings, the right scene. Still, she wouldn't have traded his expertise for her solitude. She moved to the edge. Above the treeline, wind slapped the rocks and raked her hair. She widened her stance and air swept between her legs. She raised her arms — there were no ropes, no restraints. Slowly, she lowered her arms. Reluctantly, she stepped back.

Later, she'd write about the challenge, and the beauty. Her readers would smell chalk and drip sweat, strain against rock, and burn in the sun. Through her words, they'd conquer the height. What she wouldn't share was the inner ache. She couldn't describe the pressure, temporarily assuaged; would never explain the broken halves of herself briefly made whole.

"It leaks through," Marj had said.

"What are you talking about?"

"The anger. You try to keep it out, but it seeps in. Just enough to make readers a little nervous. Most people mistake it for enthusiasm."

In the months before her decision to leave

Bryanna, Marj's comment on her writing had been, "A little angrier than usual." And they'd been selling more issues than ever.

Bryanna was waiting when she hiked into camp. "Amelia! I expected you hours ago." Her cheerful tone was forced. "Did you go climbing?"

"That's why I came up here. To climb."

Bryanna's eyes were a swamp. Fear and hope poked up like reeds. Amelia saw bitterness, too, and realized with a jolt that it had always been there.

Self-contained, Bryanna had called her, making it sound like an accusation. "Open yourself to me, baby," she'd say. "I want to touch you on the inside, too."

"You're inside now," she teased as they made love.

"I can only get skin deep," Bryanna complained. "You're holding back."

Amelia rubbed faster, building friction. Then she seized Bryanna, taking control. She knew how she liked it — fingers deep, pumping hard.

"I want —" Bryanna gasped. But Amelia barricaded the words behind a frenzy of physical touch. "Marry me," Bryanna groaned, gripped by orgasm. The pain in her eyes turned liquid; her passion dripped into Amelia's palm.

And Amelia, fueled by self-control, had whispered, "Yes." Months later, strength evaporated into safety. It wasn't a feeling she enjoyed.

In her mind, she'd been in a different bed, feeling

a different body. When she arched, seeking contact, the touch was gone. She would lie absolutely still and will it to return.

"You look exhausted," Bryanna said. "How about a shower and some hot food?"

"Food first. I'm starving."

The cabins were set in a half-circle below the treeline. Beyond the ridge, peaks rolled through the notch. In the mountains, spring hadn't made up its mind to settle; most trees showed more branch than bud. But sturdy evergreens made a rustic backdrop, and lithe birches were elegant in any season. Bryanna pointed out the main lodge, in the center of the clearing, and the bathhouse. Amelia guessed that the smaller sheds, nestled in the trees, were for storage. Bryanna's cabin was the last in line.

"Did you park at the ridge camp trailhead?"

Amelia shook her head. "I came up the other side."

"You did what?"

"That's where the good climbs are."

"For Goddess' sake, you must have been hiking for hours."

"Yeah. Is the offer for dinner still open? I could use a good meal."

"Oh, poor baby." Bryanna's sympathy translated into efficient movement. She tugged the pack from Amelia's back and propelled her toward the lodge. "You're going to love the food. It's all vegetarian — did I tell you?"

Amelia bit her tongue.

The main building housed a dining room, kitchen

and common area. Bryanna hovered while she dished up lentils, rice and limp vegetables. A rowdy dishwashing shift was underway in the kitchen.

"Most of us already ate." Bryanna led her to an empty table. "There's a beautiful ceremony every evening. When you see it, you'll know why the camp is called Sunset Ridge."

Amelia picked at her food, then pushed the plate away. "I have trail mix in my pack."

"I can do you one better." Bryanna lowered her voice. "I've got chocolate."

Amelia tried to smile. "You're on."

"We'll do the ceremony first. It's time."

"You go ahead. I'll watch."

Bryanna began to pout but another woman called to her, pulling her away. They linked arms and sashayed into the clearing. Amelia watched as the women formed a circle and began to sway. Drummers, perched on rocks, sent music tumbling. The mountains were old, peaks worn to rounded caps. Between winter and spring, bare surfaces glistened. When storms descended, there was no place to hide. Each year novice hikers, stranded away from shelter, suffered hypothermia. Some died. It was the kind of danger Amelia appreciated — open and direct.

When the chanting began, she sought the kitchen's relative quiet. She found bread and cheese and a bottle of juice. Back on the porch, she chewed methodically while the chanting pitched higher. Above the ridge, sunlight flattened and shadows lengthened. She brushed her arms, trying to wipe away the chill. She made her way to the cabin and gathered her toiletries, retreating to the showers. In a stall of solar-heated water, she scrubbed away dirt. Steam hugged her body. Fatigue, and a feeling of loneliness, lingered.

Bryanna was waiting when she came into the cabin. "You disappeared."

"I took a shower. You offered, remember?" She dressed quickly, aware of Bryanna's eager gaze.

"How about some chocolate?"

"Sounds great," she lied.

A couple banged into the cabin, laughing, hips bumping. They fell on a bunk, kissing sloppily.

"Come on," Bryanna said. "I know a place."

Amelia pulled on a sweatshirt, relieved to be outside. Behind the cabin, camp noise was muted by swishing pines. A quarter moon tipped over the trees, silver-white, like a slice of birch.

Bryanna sat on a stone bench and began peeling tinfoil. "This is Dutch milk chocolate." She giggled. "I bought a pound of it at the gourmet market. It's so creamy." She broke off generous chunks.

Amelia sat down. "Suddenly I feel spiritual." The candy should have spread like butter on her tongue. Instead, it clumped like wax. She dropped it on the bench.

"What's wrong?"

"I'm not hungry."

Bryanna said, "You're not coming back, are you?"

"No."

"I thought it would be different here. Outdoors. I wanted to share something with you, to bring us closer."

Amelia sighed. "The relationship didn't work for me."

"Why do you insist on being alone?"

"It's not like that. I just need something else."

"Something . . . or someone?"

She hesitated. Above the camp, trees wove a cross-hatch pattern. Moonlight sifted through. She said softly, "I want to be with someone I can let inside."

Bryanna gasped. "You're seeing someone. I knew it. You busy slut."

Stung, Amelia said, "Cut it out."

"I gave you everything."

"No, you didn't. But I'll give you credit for trying. It's over. How many times are you going to make me say it?"

Bryanna said curtly, "You've said enough."

Amelia got up. "I'm out of here."

Bryanna caught her at the cabin. "Baby, I'm sorry. You took me by surprise. I mean, you didn't exactly give me any warning. Don't leave like this."

She was stuffing clothes into her pack. "I'm not sleeping here."

"What are you going to do? It's dark and you didn't even bring a tent. Be reasonable. You can't hike down now. You'll get hurt."

"I'm going to roll my sleeping bag under a tree. At first light, I'm hiking out." She said wearily, "Don't call me again."

She'd spent a restful night, under the moon, away from Bryanna, and left the camp before the other women were up for breakfast. Most campers going to Sunset Ridge parked at the camp turnout, a mere three quarters of a mile from the retreat. Amelia had left her Jeep at a remote turnout, closer to her climbing site. Coming from the camp, it was a long hike, but worth it. On her way down the mountain, she stopped to do another climb. When she finally reached her Jeep, daylight was fading. She'd exhausted her trail food, and weariness was competing with the feeling of exhilaration that a good climb always left.

She wanted to write about the cliffs — the granite, sun-baked or rain-streaked, rising into a gray-white sky. Impenetrable. But climbers crawled in. With gritty fingers and sticky soles, they eeled into crannies and fissures. They didn't just scale the surface. They got deeper; climbing got them closer to the hard center.

She pulled off her pack. As for writing about the retreat, *bring a tent* and *carry your own food* were phrases that came to mind. She unlocked the Jeep. With any luck, she'd find granola bars in the glove box.

She stretched, letting her head tip back. Above the trees, pink light was fading to midnight blue. Then the sky exploded. Behind her fluttering eyelids, the night turned violently white, and erupted into lightning-streaked black.

Amelia heard herself moan and opened her eyes. In her unfocused vision, something shimmered. She thought she saw wind chimes. They twinkled and vanished.

She opened her eyes again and tried to move. The earth lurched and rolled. Sickened, she lay still. Something hard pressed her face, making it throb. A rock. It hurt, but moving hurt more. Water dripped. She wondered when it had started to rain. A rank odor filled her nostrils. Alcohol. Overhead, the wind chimes winked. She watched them, concentrated on their shape. They turned into keys.

She was on the floor of her Jeep. Above her face, the car keys dangled and beer dripped off the dash. It dribbled into her mouth, yeasty and warm. She inhaled, swallowing beer-stained saliva. She heaved, retching, and the Jeep rolled. Her head hit the floor. Light disappeared.

Chapter 12

At ten o'clock on Wednesday night, June was dozing on her couch. She knew she should undress and go to bed. She opened her eyes, hoping to hear Gretchen's soft tread. But she was alone tonight.

The phone rang, and Shane said, "We have a body. Get in here."

His urgent tone brought her fully awake. She was reaching for her gun harness before the handset hit the cradle.

She met him in his office. "There was one shot to the back of the head. The body was moved before it was dumped, and it's been there for at least ten days. Colt was right about that part. The kidnappers never intended to negotiate."

"Why risk a murder?" June asked. "Do you still think they're trying to send a message to Good Sam?"

"That's Colt theory. I'm not so sure. All the other kidnappings that we know of have been precise, with ransom payoffs that run like clockwork. We're dealing with a regionally diverse group, and they've been pulling in cash like vacuum-dust. That takes sophisticated planning. Why risk it all on a vendetta against Good Sam?"

June shook her head. "Good Sam is a phantom. No one can find her." She asked, "Does the press know about the murder?"

"They're swarming on the sheriff in charge of the local investigation. We'll take a Bureau car. Do you want coffee?"

"No. Where're we going?"

"New Hampshire. The White Mountains."

It was after one a.m. when they reached the town of Littleton. The sheriff's office had already issued a press statement, but a few reporters still prowled outside, alert for action, like lean wolves. Cal Sanders, the Grafton County sheriff, had the compact, square-muscled body of a weight lifter and the consonant-clipped, long-vowelled drawl of the north country.

"Here." The word expanded to two syllables. "These are logging roads." His finger stabbed the map. "There's an access road here, and one over here." The finger hopped. "The rescue squad found the body in national forest. There's a couple of camps, one to each side of the mountain, on private land. All the hiking trails are marked by the AMC — that's the Appalachian Mountain Club. This time of year, it's packers and climbers. It's too early in the season for the squeaky sneaker families." The drawl showed no sign of letting up.

June interrupted. "Those camps you mentioned. Who's up there?"

The sheriff changed gears in slow motion. "Like I said, outside of the national forest, it's private land. There's a women's camp, and around the bend, the survivalists. Some folks are saying militia, because they salute the stars and stripes." A grin carved a canyon on his jaw. "Toy soldiers. They like to line up and play march."

June said, "I take it the toy boys are using real fire power?"

"Up here, ma'am, so long as no one shoots a rabbit out of season, a man's guns are his own business."

Shane moved around the desk. "About those camps, Cal. Show me on the map."

June gritted her teeth. Four minutes flat, and Shane was on a first-name basis.

The sheriff reached for a mug. "Any coffee drinkers?"

"You bet."

Was it her imagination, or had Shane begun to drawl? She was closest to the coffee pot. She passed a Styrofoam cup to Shane. The sheriff glanced in his mug, shrugged and held it out. She winced as she poured fresh coffee over the scummy remains in his cup. She poured a cup for herself, trying to feel hospitable. It had an after-taste like potting soil.

The sheriff saw her grimace. "Is she a gourmet?"

Shane nodded, willing to become a mountain man at her expense. "Finicky," he agreed. "Two sugars, please." He held out his cup.

She fished real sugar cubes from a jar. "Cremora, Sheriff? Sweet'n Low?" She handed him a paper packet but didn't let it go. "Next time, sir, you wash that mug before I fix your coffee." She relinquished his sweetener.

"Yes, ma'am."

"All right." Shane's tone had returned to normal. "Tell us the rest of it."

The sheriff sipped his coffee and gave a grunt of satisfaction. "I took a call at seven-thirty. A driver noticed a vehicle off the road, up in the notch. Luckily, he had a cell phone. Some lady hiker drove half off the ridge. The only thing that stopped her going all the way down was her face on the brakes. We got the fire and rescue up, and one of the boys had to relieve himself. He took a light into the woods and damn near pissed on the body. Pardon me, ma'am. When the coroner separated the watch from the wrist bone, there was a name engraved. I ran it through NCIC and it came up a match for your missing banker." He buried his nose in his mug. "Good thing we got funded for new computers."

Shane asked, "Did you protect the area?"

"Sure. We got tape up and tagged the location of the body." He said cheerfully, "The fire and rescue trampled things pretty good getting the girl out. It took an hour to winch her Jeep."

A sick feeling twisted in June's stomach, a

sensation that had nothing to do with the sheriff's bitter coffee. She said, "I'd like to see that accident report."

Something in her tone induced the sheriff to move quickly. "There was no next of kin to notify, just an employer. I made the call when I got off the mountain. Ten o'clock."

At the top of the form, Amelia Wright's name was already neatly typed. June turned to Shane. "Get him to round up the rescue squad. Keep the car, just get me transport to the hospital." To the sheriff she said, "Notify your personnel that we'll be conducting interviews."

Shane said, "I was just about to give those orders."

June's beeper chirped. She looked at the readout but didn't recognize the number. She picked up the sheriff's phone.

"June Gavin," she said, when the line was answered.

"June? Thank God. It's Marj MacMichael. I tried your home number and your car phone."

"Are you with Amelia?"

"Do you know about the accident? Get up here."

"I'm at the sheriff's station. I'm on my way."

The sheriff was on his feet, head wagging between June and Shane. "What's this about?"

"I'll fill you in," Shane said. "Right now, Agent Gavin needs a car."

In the sheriff's outer office, a young man in uniform lounged against the wall. The clock over his head said two a.m. Coffee sent steam swirling toward his lips. June held her credentials between the cup and his nose.

"You're with me. Let's go."

"Ma'am." He pushed away from the wall, his movements as languid as his drawl. He was a gawky kid, Adam's apple rising under a clean-shaven chin.

Her glare met him square at eye level. "Name."

His spine stiffened. "Hollander."

"You're on my watch, Hollander. Coffee break is over."

His eyes widened, then his cup made a wet arc into a wastebasket. He caught up with her outside, pointing to a car with light bars on top, the county seal on the door.

"Take me to the hospital. I want speed."

"No disrespect, ma'am." He fumbled with his keys. "The body's at the morgue. You in a rush?"

"Accident victim, female." She forced the words through gritted teeth. "They winched her Jeep off the mountain. Did you hear about it?"

"Yeah. She's unconscious. Drunk driving."

"Deputy Hollander, welcome to attempted homicide. Now drive very fast."

From the outside, Littleton Hospital was quiet. Inside the brightly lit corridors, there was a low hum of activity, a subdued hush. Night staff went about their business with casual efficiency. June wanted to run. She settled for rapid strides.

Marj had commandeered the triage desk. Under a designer sweat suit, her bulk quivered. "This wasn't an accident, but no one in this do-little town will listen to reason." She steered June toward an elevator. "She's in intensive care."

158

A nurse blocked them at ICU. "I'm sorry but you can't —"

"FBI. Call the attending physician. Now."

The nurse punched an intercom, her eyes darting from the monitors to June.

"This way." Marj pulled her toward a glass-partitioned cubicle.

Inside, the air was flat, odorless, as though antiseptic had cleansed everything, even smell. Stainless surfaces gleamed dully; invasive tubing crowded the bed. Oxygen hissed. Hovering monitors showed signs of life; beneath them, Amelia lay unmoving.

A crisp voice announced, "We don't entertain visitors at this hour."

June looked at Amelia a moment longer, then turned to wage a battle of professional wills. She found herself staring at a willow-thin woman in a white lab coat, her silver hair cropped short. Blue eyes sparkled behind bifocals. June read the name tag.

"Dr. Saks. I'm Special Agent Gavin, Federal Bureau of Investigation."

"Little Jeffy Hollander is parading around my emergency department, all puffy with self-importance. To what do I owe this intrusion?" She smiled disarmingly.

June said stiffly, "I'm investigating the circumstances of Ms. Wright's accident."

"I see. In my office, if you don't mind."

The tiny consultation room held a desk, two chairs and a screen for viewing X-rays.

Dr. Saks offered Marj a handshake. "I'm sorry I wasn't available when you arrived. I've been on the

phone with the lab. I treated Ms. Wright when she
was brought in. Are you family?"

"Amelia works for me, and I have power-of-
attorney."

"Very well. And Agent Gavin is here at your
request?"

"You'd better believe it."

The doctor activated the light screen and secured
several X-rays. Darkened orbs stared from a grayish
skull.

"Ms. Wright suffered a concussion, and she's
unconscious, as you saw. We took neck and skull
films." She smiled at Marj. "The C-spine is negative.
No broken vertebrae. The initial CT scan gave no
indication of hematomas or intracranial swelling. At
the very least, there's a linear nondepressed skull
fracture, which shows up on the posterior film." She
indicated an X-ray. "That doesn't necessarily mean
neurological damage, but I've called for a consult.
There was also a nasty cut on the back of her head.
From the CBC, we know she lost a fair amount of
blood. And of course we did a blood alcohol level."

Marj was vehement. "She wasn't drinking."

"As a matter of fact, she wasn't. I just got the
test results and faxed them to the sheriff. He claims
the car was dripping beer. There was vomit, too, but
that was also negative for alcohol. Nausea is a
common side effect of concussion."

"She doesn't drink," Marj repeated fiercely.

"I'm sorry you were misinformed. Whoever was
drinking, it wasn't Ms. Wright."

"Finally." Marj crossed her arms.

June asked, "How soon will she regain
consciousness?"

"At this point, we can only wait and observe." She shut off the screen. "The rescue crew told me they found climbing equipment. It's possible that your friend took a fall, tried to drive home and became disoriented."

"She's an expert —"

June put a hand on Marj's arm. "A climbing fall doesn't explain the beer."

"Of course, if she fell," the doctor continued, "I'd expect a lot of skin abrasions, bloody scrapes on the arms and legs, possibly fractures to other areas of her body. The injuries Ms. Wright sustained are localized, mostly to the head and face. That's not what we usually see in a climbing fall."

June asked, "Can you tell from the head wound what caused the fracture?"

Dr. Saks glanced at Marj.

"Answer the question," Marj directed. "And don't mince words."

"Agent Gavin wants to know if your friend was knocked out as a result of the accident, or if someone bashed her on the back of the head first."

Marj flinched. "Well?"

"I cleaned a lot of grit out of her scalp before I stitched it. Some of it was deeply embedded, even though the wound bled profusely. I've seen heads that've been hit by rocks. The skin looks like shredded wheat." Marj paled. "That accident was no picnic," Dr. Saks said. "But the only thing I can be sure of is that the beer was poured over, not into Ms. Wright."

June stood. "I'd like to be notified as soon as she wakes up."

"You're welcome to use the doctor's lounge.

161

Pardon my saying so, but you both look like you could use some sleep."

The sympathetic tone unnerved her. June said, "I'm fine."

"Call off the goonies in ICU," Marj said. "I'm staying with Amelia. I've got a laptop in my car. I just need to get my briefcase."

The doctor's gaze lingered on Marj's retreating figure, then she beckoned to June. "Come on. I'll show you the lounge."

The square floor tiles in the old part of the hospital reminded her of high school. The halls were deserted, like corridors after the tardy bell. Clipchart-toting, stethoscope-dangling personnel went about their business in the modern wing. Only an abandoned gurney reminded June that she was in a hospital, not following the school nurse to the principal's office. Her mother had come for her at school. So they could go to the hospital. So she could visit her father before he died.

The doctor's lounge consisted of a couch, a cot, coffee and soda machines. There was a phone on the wall.

Dr. Saks said, "I have paperwork to do."

"Call me the minute there's any change."

"Of course I will." She left her alone.

June called the sheriff's station and spoke to Shane.

He asked, "How's Wright?"

"Concussed and unconscious. Shane, Amelia came up here to visit Bryanna Waters."

"You still think the girlfriend's involved?"

"I'd like to know where she was yesterday

162

evening. If she's in the mountains, I'll find her. But get someone in Boston to check her house."

"Will do. I'm about to interview a bunch of very sleepy volunteer firemen. We can't get up the mountain until dawn. Another few hours yet."

"I'd like to stay at the hospital."

"Stay in touch, Gavin. I want you close to me on this." He hung up.

She kept a vigil over the purring vending machines. The cot was tempting. After a while, she stole a pillow and stretched out on the couch. As usual, she was too long. She turned on her side. Shades were drawn over high windows. She wondered if they were ever raised. People came to this room to force themselves awake or to fool themselves into sleep, regardless of the daylight hours. She lay back, willing Amelia to wake up, even as she drifted to sleep.

The plane landed, circled on the tarmac. Emergency trucks raced to meet it. The hostage rescue team was already in place; negotiators were in the control tower, eager for contact. The plane rumbled, caught in a cross-fire of sirens. On a fire truck, June lay flat under lengths of hose, watching through a high-powered scope. The airport's rescue personnel had been removed. Hard-hatted, rubber-booted agents, their armored vests hidden under water-proof jackets, drove the fire trucks. June's sights remained fixed on the plane, its dull, oblong body unmarred by the viciousness within.

Her headset hummed, then issued toneless commands. "Rescue vehicles, hold position. Repeat, hold position."

The truck beneath her slowed, then stopped; the plane taxied closer. Shades covered every window. The aft door cracked open. Her finger remained on the trigger guard, completely relaxed. Her rifle scope magnified the co-pilot's face, stiffly professional even though a gun touched the back of his head.

"Emergency personnel," came the order. "Evacuate the runway."

Yellow-jacketed agents jumped from the trucks. From the front of the plane, an automatic weapon made one report. One man fell, his hard hat unable to staunch a bloody geyser. She saw it peripherally, her eye still focused through the scope, finger now relaxed on her trigger. The noise on the radio didn't concern her. The plane continued to taxi. On the ground, a brave man swung his companion to his shoulder, releasing the hat that dangled from a lifeless chin. He tossed it away as he ran.

June remained motionless. Beside her, the dead man's hat rocked on the hoses, the clang of it hitting her scope still ringing. Her sight picture hadn't changed. She could still see the co-pilot's rigid expression. But now she couldn't trust her aim. She didn't know if her scope had been knocked out of alignment, couldn't be sure of the bullet's trajectory. One misplaced shot might kill the co-pilot. Errant fire would send the hijackers scurrying to detonate a bomb. She flexed her finger. There was no way to be sure.

Slowly, she eased the useless weapon out of

position. Moving in fractional increments, she slipped her Browning from its holster.

The headset barked the order she'd been waiting for. "Position one, you are clear."

She stared at the plane, her unmagnified vision bringing faces into focus. The aircraft still turned through an arc, the nose rolling farther away, the aft door swinging closer. She waited, counting the meters. The plane inched around, then stopped. She swore silently, judging one hundred meters. Standard competition distance was fifty. She held her breath as the plane began to move again. She counted ninety. Eighty. She raised the handgun and released the safety.

The hijacker wore a beard, a mouthful of yellow teeth nestled in its grubby mass. Ignoring the frantic radio, she extended her arm and aligned her sights. The plane had stopped again. She'd ceased to watch the co-pilot. The only thing that mattered was target, and the gap. When the beard-filled gap filled her vision, when it was all she saw, she squeezed the trigger, and watched a nine-millimeter hole appear between hostile eyes.

Then the plane exploded. She rolled, trying to get away. Flames shot toward her like a living arm, fingertips white hot. She twisted, wrenched herself away. Then she was falling, and the fire screamed around her like an airplane's jet engine.

She landed on the floor. She put an arm across her eyes, trying to block the room's fluorescent glare.

A pleasant voice said, "It's a good thing you didn't take the cot. It's farther to fall." June looked up into concerned blue eyes. Dr. Saks was bending over her. Skilled fingers probed the back of her scalp. "Nothing tender? Good. I'm not eager to treat another concussion."

She sat up, away from the gentle hands. "I'm okay. It was just a bad dream. What time is it?"

"Four a.m. There's been no change." June eased herself back to the couch. Dr. Saks said, "There are safer ways to cope with job stress. Do you fall out of bed often?"

"Not since I got a king-size bed. After I've untangled the sheets, I get up and drink vodka."

The doctor dropped change into the soda machine. "Buy you a drink?"

"Thanks." She accepted a clammy can.

"Want to talk about it?"

"That depends. Are you a head-shrinker?"

"I'm an ER doc. That means I'm pretty good at a little of everything."

"And a specialist at nothing?"

"Oh, I guess that's one way to look at it. On the other hand, I pride myself on my broad range of experience. Up here, we get climbing falls in summer, skiing accidents in winter. The real problem, though, is alcoholism. Grafton County has one of the highest rates in the country. It's a long winter."

The soda wasn't cold enough. "Why do you work here?"

The doctor swung her legs up onto the cot. "Toss me that pillow if you're not using it." She pushed it behind her back. "I spent a lot of years at a teaching hospital in Chicago. After all the trauma and big-city traffic, I figured I deserved some fresh air. I love to hike and I can hold my own on cross-country skis. Long winters don't bother me." She smiled. "What kind of vodka?"

"Russian. Ice-cold."

She nodded. "Tell me about your nightmare."

June shook her head. "I'm sorry, Dr. Saks, but you don't know what you're asking. My nightmares are pretty sick stuff."

"Call me Rachel. I imagine you've seen a lot of sickening things. If I had to guess, I'd say evil and violence as well."

"It was a long time ago, while I was based at Quantico." She looked at the doctor. Talking was so tempting. It was also a bad idea. She sighed. All she wanted was to leave a little of the horror behind. She was tired, and Gretchen's vodka was far away. She set down the soda can and wiped her palms on her slacks. "You said you worked in Chicago?"

"That's right."

"I was there with the hostage rescue team. I shot a hijacker." It was a simple statement. "I thought the plane exploded. I know it didn't, but when I shot him, I saw fire. I practically forced a resident to show me the autopsy report. He thought I was crazy. No burns, just one bullet in the brain."

"The story was legend. Everyone at the hospital heard about it. Your picture was in the paper."

June didn't look up. "What did you hear?"

"Nothing about burns, I can assure you. We were far more impressed with your marksmanship."

"My father was a fighter pilot. I inherited his eyes, and he taught me to shoot."

Rachel asked, "What did he do after the war?"

"He was a forest ranger. He took all kinds of risks to fight fires. Wherever the hot spot was, he'd be there." She crossed her arms. "He abused me sexually. Then he had the decency to die of lung cancer. I have his dreams — he dreamed about fire, too. The night he died, he told me it had gone inside."

She had sat by his bed. When her mother left the room, he pulled her close. "I can't fight it anymore."

"You have to fight, Daddy. You have to." She used a cloth to bathe his face.

He gripped her hand. "What do you see?"

She answered as she always had. "I see the gap."

He coughed. "It's full of fire."

Her mother had returned and pushed June aside.

"Did you believe him?" Dr. Saks asked.

"He told me that some people can walk into a fire and it never touches them. You start your own fire, and the blaze breaks around you."

"Sounds like an old forester's myth."

"In my dreams, he dies in a fire." She coughed. "It's bad enough I have to remember what he did to me. I wake up every night remembering all the god-awful things that happened to him."

"He taught you to use your talent, which you enjoy. You've used your skill to save lives."

June's tone was deadly. "Am I cured yet?"

"I'm just trying to understand."

"I've spent my whole career avoiding people like you."

"I'm not surprised." Rachel shrugged. "Everyone has two shoe boxes in the closet. One is memories you want to keep, the other is the stuff you have to throw away. People spend their whole lives sorting out those boxes."

"I remember too much."

"You inherited his eyesight. You're still entitled to your own life view."

"Keep going, doc. Insight doesn't count unless you hit the diagnosis."

"Do you want a diagnosis?"

"Do you have one?"

"Trauma. I'll never understand why people in your profession think you're immune. You've got so many layers of it they bleed into each other."

"I thought you weren't a shrink."

"I meant what I said. I do a little of everything."

June put her head in her hands. "For heaven's sake. I thought if I finally told someone, I'd feel better. I feel like an idiot." Rachel laughed. June glared at her. "When did all the sympathy evaporate?"

"You'd be more pissed if I felt sorry for you. Look, I'm not telling you this is easy. I'm just saying it's enough to take out the trash. You don't have to keep trying to kill it."

June stared, unseeing. She was twelve years old, and every ounce of her concentration was focused on a competition target. Her father watched her take aim. Hitting the bull's-eye was everything. Why had she thought that shooting the target would save them?

She sighed. "What about my hallucination?"

Rachel rested her chin on her knees. "Do you want a technical answer or a practical one?"

"Practical."

"Am I on fire right now?"

"No."

The doctor raised her soda can. "Drink plenty of liquids. Try water or warm milk at night instead of vodka. You'll sleep better."

A pager sounded. She reached for hers but Rachel had already picked up the phone.

"We'll be right there." She said, "Amelia Wright is conscious."

June paused at the door. She said quickly, "Thanks."

Rachel touched her arm, then they were hurrying through the corridors, back to the modern unit.

Marj waved them into ICU. Amelia's eyes were open. Dr. Saks flashed a penlight in her eyes, and directed her to squeeze fingers and wiggle toes. June waited impatiently. Finally, the doctor picked up the chart.

June sat on the bed. "Hi." Amelia's cheeks were sunken, bones jutting like ridges under her eyes. Bruises had begun to darken. June almost reached for her but checked herself. "I need to ask you some questions." Brown eyes, hazy with pain, focused on her. "Did you hike to the women's retreat?"

Amelia started to nod. Immediately, she stiffened and held still. Her tongue edged over puffy lips. Dr. Saks adjusted the IV.

"I went to the camp." Her voice was scratchy but audible.

"Did you go rock climbing?"

"Yes."

"Did you fall?"

Behind the pain, June saw a flash of irritation. The answer was emphatic. "No." She shut her eyes.

When they opened again, she looked disoriented. "It's blurry."

"Blurry vision." Dr. Saks nodded. "That's from the concussion. You may have some dizziness, too. The neurologist will run more tests." She said to June, "Let's wrap this up."

"Amelia, did you meet someone at your Jeep, after you went climbing?"

She was quiet for a while. June thought she hadn't heard, then Amelia muttered, "I don't remember."

Dr. Saks asked gently, "What's the last thing you remember, before the hospital?"

There was another pause. "Car keys."

June asked quickly, "Were you driving?"

"I don't remember." A spasm twisted her face. "Bryanna —"

Marj stepped up. "If that hussy did anything to hurt you, I'll —"

Dr. Saks cut in. "That's enough."

"The sunset."

"What did you say?" June inched closer.

"I remember . . . the sunset. I never got in the Jeep." Her eyelids fluttered.

"Time's up," the doctor said.

June's lips touched Amelia's ear. "I'll find whoever did this. No one's going to hurt you again." She faced the doctor. "I'm posting a guard." She left the room and returned with Hollander. "No one in or out of ICU without approval from Dr. Saks or myself. Do you understand? No orderlies, no flower deliveries."

"Yes, ma'am."

Rachel was conferring with a nurse.

Marj met June's gaze. "BJ's horsepacking in

Colorado. If he harms one inch of that beautiful body, I'm going to dismember him. God," she grumbled, "I need a danish."

Dr. Saks closed Amelia's chart. The look she gave Marj was full of compassion. "Our cafeteria has a great pastry selection, so long as you like stale doughnuts."

June left them to their breakfast and called Shane.

He asked, "Are you ready to go hiking?"

"I need a map."

"I've got it all." His confidence cut through her fatigue. "This is one hell of a depressing town," he said cheerfully. He didn't wait for her to comment. "I'll pick you up."

Outside, June's breath disappeared into mist. Dawn was struggling to break through a low cloud cover. The sky was still dark. The surrounding mountains hulked, gray and brown, like squatting hounds. Cold drizzle pricked her face and saturated her thin suit jacket. It wasn't the sort of gentle rain that showered on Boston in May. The mountain air was cold, and the moisture made it raw. Fortunately, it was pollen-free. Gratefully, she inhaled the fresh air. She jumped back as Shane drove two tires on the curb, like a novice valet. Sloppy driving was the only sign he gave of being tired.

The defroster was humming to fend off the mist. The streets were mostly empty. A few early pedestrians had their flannel collars turned up. They drove past a diner and a movie marquee.

Shane said, "This town's got one of everything. One liquor store, one Rexall Drug, one juvenile delinquent."

June pointed to a satellite dish. "I bet they get all the movie channels."

He grinned. "Geographically, this region is whiter than the Southwest, smaller than the Midwest, but not as poor or as mean as Appalachia. Not very distinctive, I'd say."

"Did your fact-finding mission extend to interviews with the fire and rescue volunteers?" she asked.

"I got a half-dozen stories from as many men. The only thing everyone agrees on is that Wright was parked on the wrong side of the mountain. If she was at the women's camp, she should have used the ridge camp turnout. The Jeep was a half-day's hike from the retreat. The other bit of news is that the access road closest to where the body was found leads to the survivalist camp. The one Cal showed us on the map."

With her sleeve, June rubbed fog off her window. "Do you think they're involved?"

"If they are, they're not being very smart. But local talent never is. Or someone may want us to think that the survivalists are responsible. Any theories on what happened to Wright?"

"Her memory is shaky, but she says she never got in the Jeep. Seems like someone decked her, dumped a bottle over her, then put the gear shift in neutral and sent her rolling."

"Nice stunt. Is the girlfriend your favorite candidate? She's not home, by the way. Just some kid named Mabel."

June said, "I'll go up to the women's retreat. You can check out the men's camp."

He made a wide turn into a motel parking lot. "Doesn't it get tiring?"

"What?"

"Doing my job and yours?"

"Is that a reprimand?"

"Conflict doesn't bother you at all, does it?" He killed the engine. "It's like background noise to you. You have the highest conflict threshold I've ever seen."

"What about you?"

"I like to slow everything down. I can hear the words and the motives like they're two different conversations. Take you, for instance. Hiding at Washington Metro for years, then suddenly you want a field posting. I thought you were a burnout."

"Why did you accept my transfer?"

"I called Bass. I thought he told you. He convinced me you were worth another chance."

"That faker. When I saw him, he acted like it was news."

Shane laughed. "He gave you a high recommendation. All you care about is hitting your target. Not fast, but deadly accurate. Naïve and gutsy. That's how he described you. I can't decide if I like the combination." He paused. "He's worried about you."

She said neutrally, "I didn't know you and Bass were comparing notes."

"Someone's been hacking into the Bureau computers."

"What?"

"I'm pretty sure that's why headquarters sent Rahman. He's dissecting the systems files, level by level, trying to find out who's doing it."

"Al's a computer nerd? He does his number-crunching by hand."

"I had a hell of a time checking. He's an intelligence research specialist."

Her mind raced. "Bass thinks Al's working for Colt." She glanced at Shane. "He thinks they're watching me."

"True enough. You can't write a Post-it note without someone paying attention."

She said through dry lips, "Why do I rate VIP suspicion?"

Shane rubbed a hand over his shaved chin. His toiletries kit sat on the seat between them. "I don't know why headquarters doesn't trust you. I do, but only because Bass threatened to cut me up for fish bait if I didn't stand behind you. Listen, Gavin. I want you to do exactly as I tell you. Al Rahman doesn't work for me, but you do. Until I know the reason behind this investigation, I want you to keep your ass in the mountains and your hands off the computer. Is that clear?"

"Yeah." Her heart was thudding dully. "Have you talked to Colt? Does he know that Bass is asking questions?"

"He knows I am. You can't shove an agent like Rahman down my throat and not expect me to cough. Colt's back at headquarters rounding up his task force." He handed her a room key and a cell phone. "Get changed, and keep the phone on your person. I want to know where you are."

She looked at her watch. It was five-thirty. The mist was clearing and the sky was light.

He said, "We'll go over the maps at breakfast."

In the motel bathroom, she gave herself four minutes under the hot spray and found clean underwear in her overnight bag. She changed into running shorts. She didn't have hiking boots. Her running sneakers would have to do. She strapped her holster over a T-shirt, loaded the Browning's clip and locked a round in the chamber. She ejected the magazine and loaded another cartridge, then secured two spare magazines on the harness. She slipped on her sweatshirt and remembered Amelia's hands tugging it over her head.

"Focus, Gavin."

Next door at the restaurant, Shane and Cal were sharing jokes, home fries and coffee. Shane pulled out a chair. An open map draped the ketchup bottle and sugar jar. A waitress brought a menu and a coffee pot.

"Tea." June waved the menu away. "A plain omelette, please, and grapefruit juice."

When her food came, the sheriff said, "Eat up. You have a lot of ground to cover."

Part III
SHELLY CATALINA

Chapter 13

Without parking or a harbor view, the tiny office building in a corner of Boston's financial district had little to offer status-conscious tenants. A carry-out bagel deli had taken over the first floor. For a half-block radius, the air smelled faintly of onions. Stock portfolios and cappuccinos disappeared into the plush interiors of neighboring skyscrapers.

Two months ago, Suni had paid a gleeful landlord to have the third floor re-wired and temperature controls installed. She'd paid six months rent in cash, even though she wouldn't need the space for that long. The landlord hadn't badgered her to sign a lease. She'd had the locks changed and a security alarm installed.

Behind her curtained windows, no clients arrived or departed; there was no place for visitors to sit. She didn't need a conference table. There were no coffee pots or water coolers, not even a spider plant. On a metal desk, a powerful computer whirred. She hadn't skimped on software. When she generated her financial reports, she wanted the data to look first-rate.

Her fingers tapped the keyboard, paused, then tap-tapped again. On the computer screen, columns of numbers scrolled. The screen cleared and filled again. She stopped typing and only her eyes moved, reading through lines of data. Once more, she repeated the commands, and the numbers tallied to the same conclusion. She opened a new window and began reading the *Boston Globe* on-line.

The story had broken too late on Wednesday night for Thursday's paper, but a posting on-line that morning gave the details. A statement issued by the sheriff's department in Grafton County, New Hampshire, reported that a body had been recovered in the White Mountains. It was identified as that of a vice president from Boston Consumer's Mutual, believed to have been murdered following his abduction two weeks ago. The bank robbery, two months ago, wasn't mentioned.

She'd done the Boston robbery for Colt's benefit. It was her calling card. *Come and get me.* All of her robberies used the same technique — break the encryption codes and create a user ID. At Consumer's Mutual, she'd stolen the money and then sent an e-mail message to Colt. She wanted to make sure she got his attention. And she'd gone into the bank itself. She wanted him to know she was on his doorstep.

Colt wanted Suni. He didn't know her by that name. But her presence in his computer files was as familiar as an afghan on the sofa. She'd been blanketing his actions for two years. First she located the banks, then she drained the accounts. But he had money flowing from so many sources she couldn't reach them all. Trying to stop Colt by robbing the bank executives that funded him was like trying to empty a waterfall with a teaspoon.

She wanted him to follow her — to Boston, and then to New Hampshire. She wanted to get close — closer than a computer program would allow. So she was going to his turf, the one place where he wouldn't want her to be, where he wouldn't want to be seen. His money was in New Hampshire; but she didn't want his money after all. She wanted him. *Here I am*, she whispered, and his operating files reverberated with the electronic echo.

The viciousness of his response surprised her. In Boston, he'd done the kidnapping for real. He hadn't tried to negotiate. An innocent bank vice president was dead; she wondered if he cared. He wanted the FBI to make the connection. Her robbery alone meant nothing. But a robbery and a kidnapping made a pattern. He wanted to find her first. Out of desperation, he'd drawn half of the picture himself.

Hope and a sense of duty, honor even, had sustained her through her search. For so many years the prospect of finding him had been the focus of her life, her livelihood. But she'd been unprepared to succeed, to learn what Edward Colt was really about.

And, like a traveler who awakens to find miles of highway gone by, she hadn't paid attention to the ground she'd covered, how far she'd gone to become like him.

There was a seductiveness in it, like a romance. She'd hunted down the details of his life and modeled herself after him, even to the point of emulating his career. Who she might have become without that obsession shaping her, she couldn't fathom. She'd been prepared to love him, had predicated her life on the belief that he could accept her. Now, with rage filling in the place where hope had fled, she only wanted to introduce herself to Edward Colt, the role model she'd cherished for so long.

At the embassy, her mother held her hand. "Chok dii," she whispered. "Good luck." Suni didn't know how much gold had been paid, how many chains that had once wrapped her mother's neck now sparkled on the white breasts of embassy wives. "Khun pa American." Her mother repeated the phrase until it echoed like a chanted prayer. American father, American father. She didn't believe it. But the passport in her hand was real.

When she was fifteen, her mother had sent her to San Diego to live with her uncle's family. They were full Thai, not half like her, and her cousins teased her, called her *foreigner, farang*. Her native language was thick on their tongues. They had American accents, modern clothes and manners. She had her mother's customs. They ate pizza. She craved tiny hot chilies soaked in fish sauce. They laughed and threw anchovies on her supper. She awakened in the night, her hands beside her head kneading lumps in her pillow. She cried, as if tears could turn the fabric to pulp, white cotton to coconut milk.

She missed sour, unripe mangoes dipped in cane sugar and salt, and sticky rice wrapped in banana leaves. Her cousins pushed her through the supermarket but she couldn't identify plastic-wrapped meat. She thought of open air stalls, the animal carcasses drained of blood but dripping protein smells.

Soon she had two languages, but always one intent. *Find him.* In school, her gaze drifted from the blackboard to the soft heads and round eyes of her classmates. It wouldn't be long before she understood how to use computers, how to search military records and conjure access codes. From Harvard to Quantico to Washington, D.C., by the time she reached FBI headquarters, her name, her credentials, were all-American.

But at the age of fifteen, in the bathroom of an American high school, she had stared at herself in the mirror and wondered if her mother had ever been anything but a Bangkok whore.

Suni returned her attention to the computer screen and began to prepare the financial reports. Account numbers lined up in one column, deposit amounts in the next. She added the deposits and listed each kidnapping ransom as a subtotal. The families of the kidnap victims had never paid a cent. The banks as institutions hadn't paid. Bank directors had collected the ransoms privately and deposited the money into their own accounts. Those were the accounts she'd robbed. In a separate column, she listed the deductions. "Money in," she murmured. She clicked the mouse. "Money out." As soon as they deposited the cash, she took it away.

The directors had also made sizeable payments to a private foundation. As it happened, it was Colt's favorite charity, giving generously to family camps throughout New Hampshire. Her screen brought up the foundation's annual report in four-color graphics. Her first table showed a list of financial contributors. Bank directors topped the list. She highlighted their names for emphasis. Her next table listed grant recipients. Money in and money out. She added a pie chart and bar graphs. Colt's cash flow paraded up one column and down the next.

Finished with the reports, she connected her modem and dialed the FBI's database. She loaded a new program. Like a stone in water, it sank to the deepest level. Beneath the databanks, under layers of programming, she delved into the Bureau's systems files. Like a snake looped through vines, virtually invisible, her program wound its way into the encryption mechanism. When the formula had been deciphered, she withdrew her program, like pulling back on a syringe. The puncture wound closed; like a needle full of serum, she had the codes. Quickly, she created an ID and fed it back into the operating system. Within moments, she was on the Bureau's computer as a legitimate user.

She knew that Colt had a systems operator trying

to track her progress. From his user ID, she knew his name was Al Rahman. But by the time he'd sifted through enough levels to find her, she was gone. Her program wasn't traceable — she removed it from the system as soon as she had the operating codes. Once she was on-line, she was one of hundreds of official users with a legitimate ID.

She went after Colt's files, and saw that he'd received updates on the Good Sam investigation. June Gavin was the agent who'd been dogging Amelia. God, the woman was thorough. Suni skimmed the reports, then stopped and reviewed the logs. Rahman was all over Gavin's files. Behind her regular documents, he'd added something. It didn't show up on the menu; Suni doubted that June knew it was there. But any systems operator would see it in a heartbeat. She bypassed the password protection and opened the file. What she saw made her breath catch. The hidden file contained ransom and robbery amounts — the whole list. The only people with that much information were Colt and Suni.

"They're setting her up," she whispered. It was a crock, but if the file was exposed, Gavin was going to look guilty. "Shit." She typed furiously, pulling up Gavin's personnel file. "Hostage rescue." HRT meant Quantico. A hero. "Not a good move, guys. Wait a sec." She scanned the page. "Employee assistance." They thought Gavin was a burnout. "No wonder." Disgruntled agents made perfect scapegoats.

Rahman knew that Gavin wasn't Good Sam. But he was doing a hell of a job making it look that way. Colt was worried. With Suni so close to New Hampshire, he needed a diversion. If he had to pull back, the brunt of an internal investigation would hit

Gavin like a freight train. The woman didn't stand a chance.

Rahman was good, if unoriginal. It was too bad they'd never have a chance to play chess. She'd win. She'd clobber him, turn the board before the game was over, give him every advantage and beat him again. She was that much better.

She deleted the file implicating Gavin, as well as the surrounding layers of code. It was like erasing a shadow. The next systems operator would see an empty pocket, akin to a black hole in cyberspace. She continued to peruse Gavin's reports. Curious, she looked up the assignment log. Poised above the keys, her fingers froze. Gavin was in New Hampshire. Suni stared at the screen. She knew Gavin wasn't involved with Colt. Moments before, her head had been on his butcher block. Suni could use her. She paused before closing the personnel file. She wondered if Gavin really was a burnout, or if she still had guts.

Suni opened a fresh box of disks and copied her carefully prepared financial report. Then she loaded a new program and set a timer. In twenty-four hours, her bar graphs, like the spine of an eviscerated animal, would surface. Scrolling through modem and fax lines, the information would reach each division director at FBI headquarters. The numbers lined up, waiting to be counted, added, compared. Her computer program would automatically send the report tomorrow. Today she had another, more private message to deliver. When Colt turned on his computer this morning, he'd find her invitation in his e-mail.

Meet me in New Hampshire. She signed it *Good Sam.*

It wasn't an alias she would have chosen for herself. But when she'd walked out of Consumer's Mutual and stepped into the alley, Amelia was there. This time Suni had surpassed Colt. She'd murdered first.

In New Hampshire, he would probably try to kill her. It was too late for him to learn, to know her as his daughter. She was a tormentor, a competitor, a robber stealing his money. She knew everything about him that he wanted to keep secret. She hated knowing. She wished she could have spent the rest of her life searching and never finding out the truth, never having to forgo the dream of an American family.

If she didn't survive the showdown with Colt, she wanted someone to know who she was. Someone who could notify her cousins in San Diego. So they could tell her mother. She wanted her mother to know that she'd tried. Suni picked up the computer disk and sealed it in an envelope.

Finished with her work, she left the computer running and walked to the window. She opened the blinds a fraction and peered out. It was still early and the streets were calm. Boston wasn't so different from Bangkok. Bangkok had more dirt, and more glitter. In a few hours she'd be in New Hampshire. Then, if she got out alive, she'd sail for Thailand.

She missed the monsoons, the way clouds quenched daylight and the air became a flood. In Bangkok, the torrential rains overflowed what was left of the canals. Streets flooded and traffic stalled. Schoolchildren, with their shoes in one hand, bookbags balanced on their heads, waded barefoot through the scum- and snake-infested water. Beyond the city's limit, free of its insanity, rice fields soaked up the rain and steamed; heat turned the water back into air.

Suni closed her eyes. She wanted to sail along the Thai peninsula and go ashore where the water was see-through blue, the sand sun-bleached white. Then, if she couldn't rest, she'd slip into the jungle and sink into a sea of green banana leaves. In her daydream, she wasn't alone. Amelia was on the boat, holding the tiller and the sails, knotting the ropes.

Suni opened her eyes. She knew that if she lived to sail for open water, she'd have to hold the sails by herself.

Chapter 14

June drove the Bureau sedan to the ridge camp turnout. She pocketed the cell phone and jogged the three-quarters of a mile uphill to Sunset Ridge Retreat.

On the scenic ridge, women milled in a clearing. A screen door slammed, and June followed several campers into a rustic lodge. She smelled breakfast cooking. Helpers in aprons bustled in and out of the kitchen. Other women sipped coffee and conversed.

"Horrible," she heard a woman say.

"Can you imagine finding someone dead in the

woods?" another one asked. "And so close to here. Just on the other side of the ridge."

They'd been listening to the radio, obviously. The press had done their job. It was already common knowledge that a body had been found.

A woman carrying pitchers of fruit juice paused. "Are you checking in? The office is through the kitchen."

On the other side of the swinging doors, June stopped, trying to decipher the meatless aromas. Zucchini bread. Pans of quiche were cooling on the stovetop. She stepped closer and sniffed. Mushrooms.

"Get your nose out of my cooking!" She looked up to see a ten-inch chef's knife waving. A skinny woman with a shaved head yelled, "Wait in line like everyone else."

She apologized to the knife. "I'm looking for the manager's office."

Sharp eyes replaced the knife tip, scanning her body. The woman crossed the kitchen. "Newcomer, huh? What's your name?"

"June. What's yours?"

"Call me Skinny." She thrust out a hand, squeezing too hard. "Office is down the hall." The knife indicated a corridor. "Hurry up. Breakfast starts in a half-hour."

The short hallway was covered in corkboard. June paused to read the notices. Spiritual retreats, yoga classes, women's canoe trips. Many of the women had posted business cards. Her eye caught Bryanna Waters' name. She felt the motion before she saw it. Skinny, a flyer in hand, was crowding against her.

"Gotta post this menu." She reached for a tack.

June thought, *I bet she grabs my ass.*

Skinny's arm dropped. And there it was, the supposedly accidental brush of a hand on her butt.

"Crowded back here." Skinny growled the words in her ear. From behind a closed door, June could hear a woman talking. Skinny said, "Wanda's on the phone." She was blocking the passage back to the kitchen.

June asked, "Do you greet all the guests?"

"Official welcome wagon, that's me." She jerked a thumb at her chest. Her other hand was empty.

"Where's your knife?"

Skinny grinned and gave a mock bow. "You're safe with me. After breakfast I'll show you around."

June stepped forward. If she took a breath, her breasts would poke Skinny's flat chest. "It's safer for you if you stay in the kitchen." Her hand flashed up, four fingers jabbing Skinny's sternum. Skinny grunted and stepped back. June grabbed her shoulders and spun her around, catching one arm and twisting. Her other hand clamped the back of her neck. Using her feet, she forced Skinny's legs apart. "Now listen to me, you emaciated little dyke. I'm not here to get hit on, so back off."

"What the hell —" Skinny sputtered. "What are you, some kind of cop?"

"If you behave yourself, I'll show you my badge."

"Let go." Skinny went limp. "I won't touch you."

"Don't fight me," June warned. She side-stepped, then released her grip.

The office door banged open. "I thought I heard somebody out here. Are you checking in?" A portly woman in an oversized sweatshirt beckoned. "I'm Wanda. Don't be shy." The motherly voice scolded, "Skinny, our guests are waiting for breakfast." Wanda

191

settled herself behind her desk and asked, "Is this your first time at Sunset Ridge? What's the name on the reservation?" She peered over the top of reading glasses. "You did make a reservation?"

June shut the office door and placed her ID on the guest register. "I don't want to upset your guests. In exchange for your cooperation, I'll be discreet." She didn't mention that she was already out-of-bounds with the kitchen help.

Wanda picked up June's credentials and examined them closely. Her glasses, when she took them off, hung from a chain on her bosom. On her sweatshirt, a fierce cat's head snarled. The lettering said, *Plymouth Mountain Cats. Thirtieth Reunion.*

"I've been the administrator at this camp for eight years," Wanda said. "I've never had any complaints or disturbances. And I don't negotiate my cooperation, I give it willingly. As for your discretion, I trust the professionalism implied by this badge." She handed back June's wallet. "May I assume you're here about the banker who was killed? It's all over the news this morning." She indicated a radio. "Some of the women were upset, but I told them not to worry. It happened across the ridge. Who do you suppose could do such a thing? And to leave him in the woods like that. It's inhumane."

June sat in a metal folding chair. "I'd like to ask you about a guest who stayed here. Amelia Wright."

Wanda flipped a page in her reservation book. "Our celebrity visitor. Oh, she wasn't a model or a star, not by a long shot. But some of the campers recognized her. She works for a fancy magazine and has an attitude problem." June folded her hands, forcing herself to stay seated. Wanda said, "She was here Tuesday night. She was supposed to stay another night, but she left before breakfast yesterday morning. Very stand-offish. And she upset one of the other guests so much that she also left early."

"Who was that?"

Wanda consulted the register again. "Bryanna Waters. A nice lady, but very emotional. I'm afraid I can't give her a refund."

"So Ms. Waters and Ms. Wright were here together?"

"They bunked in the same cabin. At least, that's what the reservation book says. I'm an early riser. It looked to me like one of them spent the night under a tree."

"Did they leave together?"

"No." Wanda was thoughtful. "The writer took off first. I believe Ms. Waters left about an hour later."

"Did Ms. Wright talk to anyone else while she was here?"

"Several guests approached her. She wasn't rude, but she never went to charm school."

"What about yesterday morning? Did you see anyone with her before she left?"

Wanda shook her head. "She was alone. I probably wouldn't have noticed, but she was hiking in the wrong direction. Everyone uses the ridge camp trail, which leads to the parking turnout. The writer was heading for the other side of the mountain. It's beautiful hiking, but aside from logging roads and cliff formations, there's nothing out that way."

June said, "I thought there was another camp, a group of survivalists."

Wanda chuckled and sipped coffee from a mug that said, *Plymouth High — Thirty Years.* "You'd think, with all the target practice they do, those boys could hit the broad side of a barn."

"Is there any contact between the two camps?"

"I don't always share the opinions of every camper, but I think, when you meet our guests, you'll see why it's unlikely that they would have much interest in the men." She smiled. "You could say the two camps are worlds apart philosophically."

"How difficult is it to get from this camp to the other side of the ridge?"

"Surely you don't think someone here was involved with what happened?" When June didn't answer, she said, "It takes several hours if you're hiking. One of the logging roads cuts straight across, though. Four-wheel drive will get you there in forty minutes. But, Agent Gavin, our guests have nothing to do with that other camp. We have nothing in common."

"Who owns Sunset Ridge?"

Wanda looked surprised. "We're a nonprofit corporation, on private land, funded by guest fees and private donations. Would you like a brochure?"

"Thanks." It was the same glossy advertisement she'd seen at Bryanna's. "Were there any other guests checking in or out during the last two days?"

Wanda sighed and flipped register pages. "Two check-outs. They left yesterday to catch a plane to New York. And I had one check-in at lunchtime. Most of our guests arrive and leave on the weekend." She looked at June expectantly. "Is there something I should know about?"

"Yesterday evening, Amelia Wright's Jeep ran off the road. Perhaps you heard about it."

"Oh, my heavens. The radio mentioned an

accident. I had no idea Ms. Wright was the driver. Is she all right?"

"She's in intensive care."

"How terrible. She wasn't here long, but I'll send a card." Wanda glanced at her watch. "I'm sorry. I wish I knew more."

As she left the office, Wanda was back on the phone. June made herself a cup of tea and sat at one of the tables. Skinny scowled at her empty plate. "I already ate breakfast," June said.

She had no trouble starting conversations about *Outdoors Woman* magazine, and many of the women recognized Amelia's name. One of the campers had heard Bryanna and Amelia squabbling, but gossip quickly turned to other topics. June walked outside and stood on the ridge.

"Why don't you spend the day, wait and see the sunset." Skinny lit a cigarette and took a drag.

June said, "I was a little rough earlier. No offense."

"None taken." Skinny sat down. "That little writer bitch. Is she your girlfriend?"

"No."

"Then why are you chasing all over camp playing twenty fucking questions. You're after something, lady cop."

The cigarette dangled from Skinny's lips as June hauled her up. "Do you know who hurt Amelia Wright?"

Skinny grinned around clamped teeth. "Far as I can see, you're the only one who wants to hurt somebody." June dropped her hands. Skinny crushed her cigarette. "Sweet Amelia. She ain't my type." Her boots scraped softly as she walked away.

When June got back to the car she opened a map. There was another access road leading to the camp. She followed it, and discovered that it was a supply road, leading directly to the storage sheds. She studied the map until she located the road that cut under the ridge. She wanted to get a look at the place where Amelia's Jeep had gone over.

It took forty-five minutes to get to the turnout that was closest to the accident site. Off the asphalt, the mountainside descended steeply. June's feet slipped and she caught herself. Tree trunks were wrapped with tattered police tape. The ground was torn up, branches broken. She whispered, "Where are you, Bryanna?"

She trudged to the trailhead and began to hike. Within half a mile she could see the rock formations at the top of the ridge. Amelia had said she'd been back at her Jeep at sunset. On the way down from the retreat, she must have stopped to climb. June stared up at the sheer granite rocks. "You're crazy, Amelia." The wind caught her words and whisked them away.

Chapter 15

The throbbing in Amelia's head had receded to background noise, an insistent bass that wouldn't quit. Tenderly, she touched her face. The swelling along her jaw and under her eyes felt familiar. Memories crowded her bed like hovering surgeons. She wondered if she had another black eye.

"How's the head?" She blinked, waiting for a blurry face to sort itself into features. "I'm Dr. Saks. Remember me? I treated you last night."

"Marj." Her voice cracked. The doctor held water

to her lips and she sipped gratefully. She tried again. "Marj was here."

"All night long. When the batteries in her laptop ran down, she took over my office. I finally convinced her to get some rest. Later today, I plan to make sure she eats something besides danish." Amelia lay still while a penlight flashed in her eyes. "The neurologist is pleased with your progress. I just wanted to have one more peek at you." Fingers pressed into her palm. "Squeeze." She tightened her grip and the doctor winced. "No problem there. Other side." Amelia squeezed again. "Right. I'm not a rock, just so you know."

"Sorry."

"Not at all." The prodding examination continued, with the doctor commenting favorably. "I think we can take you off the critical list. You'll be sore for a while, and there may be some lingering headaches and dizziness. If they persist, or if the nausea returns, see a doctor. I also want you to see a doctor if you feel weakness in any limbs, or if you experience hearing problems. I'll refer you to a specialist in Boston."

"June."

"She's certainly a specialist, but not in medicine."

Her head was pounding. She tried to tune out the doctor's chatter. "Where's June?"

Dr. Saks opened her mouth but the answer never left her lips. A shockwave reverberated through Amelia's skull. A uniformed body flopped into the room and thumped to the floor. Above it was a hand with a gun. Amelia struggled to sit up but the effort only brought her closer to the gun. Then it disappeared behind a flap of white. The doctor pushed her back, held her down. Somewhere outside, at the nursing desk, maybe, someone screamed. When the gunshot came, she recognized the sound. Dr. Saks was no longer blocking her view, but Amelia wasn't looking at the gun. She stared at the white jacket. Slowly, the lab coat changed colors, inch by blood-soaked inch.

On the mountain trail, June's cell phone rang.

She answered, "Gavin."

Shane said, "The sheriff just got a call. Shots were fired at the hospital."

She steeled herself, and asked, "Amelia?"

"I don't know yet. We're on our way."

She ran for the sedan. Gravel flew as her tires spun out. She raced for the hospital.

Reporters were clustered at the entrance. She shoved her way though, knocking into a man with a TV camera on his shoulder.

He grunted, "Watch it."

She pushed past him.

A uniformed man intercepted her at the gift shop. "Agent Gavin?"

"Where's your boss?"

"ICU."

A hospital guard had replaced the duty nurse. Monitor screens were silent; the patients had already been moved. On a gurney, a body lay covered. She lifted the sheet. Hollander.

"He asked to stay on for an extra shift." The sheriff's eyes were gray and unforgiving. "He took it in the heart. One of the bullets tore through his hand, probably when he tried to grab the gun." He carefully replaced the sheet. All traces of country charm had vanished. The northern accent no longer drawled but sounded terse. "Dr. Saks was late getting off the night shift again. She's in surgery. They told me she'll be lucky if she only loses a kidney."

"Cal, I'm sorry." She asked, "Amelia Wright?"

"Funny thing. They shot two locals, then carried her right out of here." The question glinted in his eyes. *Why not shoot her, too?*

Shane was stooped over bloody linen. He looked up. "Agent Gavin, Sheriff Sanders. We'll use the conference room."

"You're not going anywhere," a determined voice said, "until I get an explanation."

Marj's clothes were fresh — expensively cut jeans and a chamois shirt. Her jogging shoes were spotless, her hair washed and styled. June issued a silent thanksgiving that Marj had been in a motel shower instead of ICU.

Marj stoically surveyed the sheet-draped gurney and bloody hospital bed. "What happened?"

June said, "Why don't you join us in the conference room."

"No civilians." Cal's tone left no room to argue.

Marj took a cell phone from her purse. "Is Amelia injured?"

June shook her head. "We don't know."

"What happened?"

"No statements." Cal glowered.

Marj activated her phone. "In five seconds, I'm calling lawyers. The press is already outside."

Cal stepped toward her, his shoulders squared.

June said, "Shane, why don't you and Cal get

started in the conference room." She led Marj away from the gurney, then took the phone. "Put this away and keep your mouth shut, or I'll let the sheriff lock you up." She waited until the phone was out of sight. "Amelia's been kidnapped. The officer assigned to guard her was killed. All we know is that she was alive when they carried her out."

"I'd like to know what you plan to do."

June matched her icy reserve. "I'm going to find her."

After a pause, Marj said, "I'll be in Rachel Saks's office. I expect a report in one hour."

June bit back a retort. "Marj." She called after her and waited for her to turn. "Dr. Saks was shot, too. She's in surgery."

Briefly, pain blanketed her face. Then her eyes resumed their calm, hard glare. "One hour."

The wood-paneled conference room amplified Cal Sanders' rage. "What in God's name did you put my people in the middle of?"

"Kidnapping." Shane leaned against the wall, seemingly unruffled. "Possibly the same group that abducted and shot the banker."

"Where the hell is Colt?" June demanded. "Why isn't his task force up here?"

"I spoke to the task force leader," Shane said. "He's convinced we're working an unrelated case. We never made a solid connection between the robbery and kidnapping. The timing was wrong, and there was never any attempt to negotiate for the release of the hostage. And we never found Good Sam. There's no evidence to support Colt's theory that Good Sam robbed the bank and knew the kidnappers. Good Sam killed a rapist in an alley behind the bank. That's it. As for Wright, we won't know who took her, or why, until negotiations begin. If it's the same group that took the banker, let's pray they want to talk this time."

"That body was found so close to the survivalist's camp. Did you talk to them?" June asked.

"I don't know what's worse — their aim or all the anti-government propaganda. They think the Fish and Game Department is evil. They're staunch supporters of the Second Amendment and they hate the FBI."

Cal's fist banged the table. "You'll blame anything on those boys up the hill. First the bank man, now this lady. We found that body on national forest land. Anyone could have driven up the road and dumped it. And he was killed with a thirty-thirty Winchester soft-tip round. That's standard hunting ammo."

"The men at that camp aren't hunting whitetails out of season," Shane said calmly. "You were up there, Cal. They've got Ruger MP-nines."

"The submachine guns the police are using?" June asked. "These guys are serious."

"I also saw belts of thirty-caliber machine gun rounds and magazines of seven-point-six-two ammo."

"What are they doing, stockpiling for a holy war?"

"They're quoting the Constitution, not the Bible. The question is, are they in the kidnapping business?"

"Are you going to get BATF involved? Alcohol, Tobacco and Firearms usually deals with these groups."

Shane said, "That's up to Colt. Even though we're

not working with the task force, he's still special agent in charge. At the moment, he's not returning my phone calls."

Cal said, "I don't care if this case is a piece of a bigger investigation or not. Someone walked in here and shot two people I care about, people I've known for years. I'm concentrating on who shot my friends, and who took the girl."

June was thinking of Hollander's stiff spine and clean-shaven chin. She hadn't had to lift the sheet very far to see the savage wound on his chest. She thought of Dr. Saks, still in surgery. Maybe it was because hospitals were so white, but the ICU had looked horribly red. She blanked her mind, then directed her complete attention to the sheriff.

"You want to know what bothers me?" He leaned into the table. "If they tried to kill her once by sending her car off the mountain, why didn't they shoot her, too, and finish the job?"

June said, "I don't think we should assume a connection between the car accident and the kidnapping."

Shane asked, "You still think it's a domestic thing with the girlfriend?

"I haven't been able to find and question Bryanna Waters. If I'm right, she's probably still in the area." She asked, "Cal, can you spare a man to run a motel search?"

He got up and punched numbers on the wall phone, gave the orders.

"All right," Shane said. "If we take the car wreck out of the equation, the question is still who kidnapped Wright and why?"

Cal crossed his arms. "Maybe the Campfire Boys

203

did it after all. Maybe they want a little insurance against you."

June faced him. "What are you saying?"

"You're swarming all over the mountain, up one side, down the other, talking about the Bureau of Alcohol, Tobacco and Firearms. You're in their face making firepower shopping lists. Begging your pardon, but no one up here likes you all that much. If I had the BAT-Fuckers on my tail, I might grab a little bargaining power, too. It wasn't hard to figure — putting a guard on Wright was like slapping on a red sticker at a tag sale." He grunted. "I should have shut them down a year ago. Freedom of speech, my ass. You can provide backup."

June was on her feet. "Not that way. You lost one man already."

"I don't need reminding. I know those boys. I can talk to them."

"You're wearing a county uniform. If they have Wright and you confront them, we'll be notifying your family tonight." She turned to Shane. "Let me go up."

"Out of the question."

"I'll take a rifle. I can get her out."

"Get it through your head, Gavin. You're not a sniper anymore. And we don't know who has Wright. Let's calm down and give them a chance to contact us. When we know who we're dealing with, we'll negotiate."

Cal was grumbling like a low speed thunderstorm. Someone knocked on the conference room door. Cal pulled it open. One of his men held out an envelope.

He examined the label, then handed it to June.

"For you. Someone slipped it in with the station's mail."

The envelope bore no postmark or postage. It was addressed to Special Agent June Gavin and said, *Urgent*. Cal handed her his pocket knife and she cut the seal. A computer disk fell out.

Littleton's Camp & Apparel looked like it had started as a shoe store and expanded into accessories. It was just before lunchtime and Suni was doing some shopping.

"Hi. Can I help you?"

Suni considered the clerk's form-fitting shorts and supple, ankle-high boots. She returned the friendly smile. "I need hiking gear. What you're wearing looks perfect."

The clerk beamed. "Shoe size?"

"Six."

"Tiny, aren't you? That's okay. We've got every size and color."

Twenty minutes later, Suni piled layers of polypropylene and cotton-wool blends onto the counter.

"Spring hiking is unpredictable," the clerk warned. "Now you're prepared for anything." She took Suni's credit card. "Are you here on vacation?"

"Yes, I'm just beginning my vacation. Do you mind if I use your dressing room to change?"

"Go right ahead." She handed back her credit card. "Thank you, Miss Catalina."

When Suni reemerged she was wearing a pink and black outfit. The boots were pink and purple.

The clerk said, "You look great. Ready for the trail."

"That reminds me. I need a map."

"Sure. Any place in particular you're hiking to?"

"Sunset Ridge."

In Dr. Saks's office, Marj gave up the computer without a word. Shane inserted the disk and began typing. He scrolled through the information twice, then printed a hard copy. Columns of numbers spilled into the tray. He printed a second copy and Marj snatched it up.

June was looking over Shane's shoulder. "What is it?"

"Bank statement," Marj said.

Shane indicated the first column of numbers. "These are the ransom amounts for each of the kidnappings in Maryland and Virginia." His finger was halfway down the list. "They're listed as deposits into separate accounts, but the totals match the ransoms."

"And these?" June pointed to the top numbers.

"Someone's been making money for a long time."

"Not lately," Marj said. "Look at the debits. The last four entries are a wash."

Cal was shoulder to shoulder with Marj. "Say it in English."

"Whoever made the deposits," Shane said, "held the funds in private accounts. Beginning two years ago, withdrawals equal deposits. That's when someone started stealing the ransoms."

Marj nodded. "Money in, money out. A wash. That's what I said."

June frowned. "The kidnappers weren't robbed. The banks were, after they paid the ransoms. Why are the ransom and robbery amounts showing on the same statement?"

Shane was staring at the numbers. "We're generalizing. We keep saying the banks paid the ransoms. Technically, the bank officers and board directors paid. They paid as individuals."

"Well, I hope they had liability insurance," Marj said.

Shane said, "It's called banker's kidnap-ransom insurance. Unless an extortion or ransom demand is made on the premises, most blanket policies don't cover kidnapping. Kidnap-ransom coverage pays if someone phones up and demands a ransom for the return of your colleague or kid."

"In that case, nobody loses but the insurance company." Marj sounded like she approved.

June met Shane's eyes. "It's insurance fraud."

He blinked. "Consumer's Mutual was the only bank that disclosed account numbers. During the robbery, the funds were transferred electronically — specifically, from the directors' individual accounts." He tapped the computer screen. "This is what your bank book would look like if you deposited a ransom, and then someone stole it from you."

June was incredulous. "The kidnappings were bogus. That's why everything went so smoothly. A bank officer disappears for a while, his colleagues pretend to pay a ransom, and then they collect against their insurance policy."

"Then someone, Good Sam, presumably, discovered the profits and began stealing them," Shane added. "That explains why the banks were so quiet. No one wanted the insurance adjuster to take a closer look."

Marj was studying the list. "The profit margin disappeared two years ago. Before that, roughly one quarter of the total deposits were later withdrawn. They're moving money. I'd love to get a look at their stock portfolio."

June scowled. "What happened in Boston? What was that all about?"

"Consumer's Mutual was never part of the scheme," Shane said. "Boston was a command performance."

It was too crowded to pace in the small office. June crossed her arms. "Why would Good Sam provoke the kidnappers? She's been making a lot of money off their insurance scam."

"Biting the hand that feeds her," Shane agreed. He studied the computer screen. "She can't get to all of their money. There are too many accounts."

June frowned at the columns of numbers. She said slowly, "Maybe Good Sam isn't just a greedy bank robber. Colt seemed to think that she was competing with the kidnappers, trying to hurt them. Maybe her motive isn't money. She wants to shut them down."

"In that case," Shane said, "chances are this disk was delivered to you compliments of Good Sam." He began typing again. "There are two more documents on here." He hit the print button and the computer whirred. The tray began filling up.

Marj snatched up several sheets. "This is an annual report. What a lousy investment plan. They gave their profits to charity. The Catamount Foundation." She rattled the page. "Stupid name. And look at this stupid logo."

The sheriff elbowed his way in. "That's a catamount. A mountain cat."

June stared at the picture of a snarling cat's head. She'd seen it twice. Once on a sweatshirt. Once on a ring.

Marj gathered up the rest of the pages. "Someone sent us the whole financial report."

June asked, "Marj, do you still have your laptop?"

"Of course. And a fresh set of batteries."

"Can you access public financial records?"

"Agent Gavin, I can access the IRS if I have to."

"And your magazine can get media archives, right?"

"What do you need?"

"Verify the financial report. Find out who supports the Catamount Foundation, and if it makes donations. I also want to know if a local town called Plymouth had any school reunions recently. If you can find it, get a guest list."

"I'm on it." She grabbed Cal's arm. "Let's go, Sheriff. I hope you can run a fax machine? And I really need a cup of coffee." He sputtered as Marj dragged him out.

June shut the office door. "Colt used Amelia Wright, and me, to try to find Good Sam. He did surveillance on Wright for two months. When that didn't work, he sent me to question her. From the beginning, he knew there was a connection between the robberies and the kidnappings. Shane, Colt's the one who wants Good Sam. He's been desperate to find her."

He stared at her. "Unless you have proof, we're not having this conversation."

"Has he called yet? Do you know where he is?"

"No." He returned his attention to the computer.

Frustrated, she slapped the edge of the desk, but held her tongue. On the computer screen, statistics began to scroll past.

She said, "That looks like a Bureau personnel file." She watched as a computerized photo appeared.

Shane positioned the monitor so she could get a better look. "Agent Gavin, meet Special Agent Shelly Catalina." He began to read off the stats. "She was born in Thailand. Her mother is native Thai. Father . . . there's no entry, but he must have been American. At eighteen, she declared American citizenship. At twenty-one, she graduated on a full scholarship from Harvard and was recruited into the Bureau's science program. Very brainy." When he got to the end of the file, he said, "She resigned two years ago. She was barely with the Bureau for a year. Either she wasn't cut out to be a special agent, or she didn't like her colleagues. It's a shame to waste that kind of training."

The door to the office banged open. Marj was juggling cups of coffee and an armload of fax paper. The sheriff was right behind her, unfolding a map.

Marj began spreading pages under Shane's blinking eyes. "The Catamount Foundation takes in a lot of money. And they give a lot of it away. Sunset Ridge Retreat gets a healthy grant each year. Here's a list of other recipients." She slapped a page on the desk. "The annual report lists major contributors. As you can see, a lot of bank officers are making generous donations to the foundation."

"What about Consumer's Mutual?" June asked.

Marj passed her a fax sheet. "It looks like you were right about that. None of the Boston directors are contributing to Catamount."

June heard rustling and turned to see Cal hanging a map from the X-ray screen. A scroll of fax paper was stuffed in his back pocket. He uncapped a pen and began circling locations.

"Cal?"

"Your Catamount Foundation makes grants to more than one campground in this state." He pointed to his circles. "One in Claremont, and one next door in Keene. Then over here," he pointed east, "in Barrington, and up here in the mountains at Sunset Ridge. Except for the Ridge, which is for women, they're all family camps."

Marj consulted one of her lists. "Those camps are private nonprofits. They're eligible for grants."

In the midst of the hubbub, June said quietly, "I'm going up to Sunset Ridge."

Marj looked at her sharply. "Do you think that's where the kidnappers are holding Amelia?"

"I think the people who run the Catamount Foundation are up there. If they've got Amelia, I'll find her, too."

Shane didn't look up. "Ms. MacMichael, did you find that information from Plymouth that Agent Gavin requested?"

"Right here." She slapped another page under his nose. "Someone better tell the nurses they're running low on fax paper."

Shane said, "It's going to take me a while to sort through all of this. I'd rather not be disturbed."

Marj pulled a second chair up to the desk. "Let me show you." Her eyes implored June.

Shane kept his head bent over the papers. June closed the office door behind her.

Outside, she was surprised to find that the afternoon was fading. The sky was gray, pregnant with moisture. The sunset was lost, the light hemmed in by clouds.

Cal caught up with her in the parking lot. "Big storm." He sniffed the air. "Can I give you a lift?"

Chapter 16

Suni leaned against a tree. She sat on her heels, her back to the trunk. The ridge was dredged in clouds and the gathering wind tasted of rain. On the ocean, she'd know the storm — when it was coming, from which direction. But the surrounding trees and rocks foiled her senses. She envied June Gavin's field experience, and Amelia's mountain know-how.

Droplets spattered through the branches and she shifted position. She'd worked hard to make a place for herself in this country. She loved its bold peaks and endless coast. She'd memorized the Constitution and absorbed the customs, learned to eat pizza and buy pre-packaged food. She'd gone all the way to the FBI to win her father's trust. Instead, she'd uncovered his crimes. Streams ran out of the mountains and joined themselves to rivers. From sea to lovely shining sea, no matter how brightly they sparkled, no matter how swiftly they coursed, for her the waters were tainted, poisoned at the source.

She heard the rumble of thunder and a different, man-made sound. As the trucks approached, Suni inched forward and crawled to the edge of the access road. The drivers unloaded and transferred crates; the cargo disappeared into the storage sheds. As she watched, they grappled with an awkward sack. It rolled in their grasp, and the human-sized bag lurched and kicked. They dragged it inside. The trucks lumbered away.

Cal parked the patrol car at the base of the access road. He shut the lights and the engine, and they sat quietly as two trucks rolled into view. At the fork, they turned up the mountain road.

He squinted. "Can't make out the tags." June read off the license plates as the first truck, then the second, turned. "Huh. Good eyes."

"Those trucks are coming from Sunset Ridge."

He nodded. "And they're heading up to the men's camp."

"I don't think they're making a fruit and salad delivery."

He reached for the keys. "Let's find out."

She stopped him. "Get backup."

"By the time I get another car up here, they'll be on private land. I'm going to pull them off the road while they're crossing through the national forest. All I need is an expired tag or a broken taillight."

"It's too dangerous. They're too heavily armed. Are you familiar with the Ruger MP-nine? It's a submachine gun."

"I don't need a firearms lesson, lady."

"Judging from the ammunition Shane saw, they probably have M-fourteen assault rifles and tripod-mounted machine guns."

He turned in his seat to face her. "If they're transporting weapons illegally, I'll put an end to it. But the last place in the world they're going to store their cache is under the fannies of a bunch of women wearing mosquito-repellant."

June stared out the window. The dusk was deepening and rain was beginning to patter lightly on the car. She said, "I thought he was just using the camps to launder money."

"You think you know who's behind the fraud, don't you?"

"I know who's running the Catamount Foundation, and I'm hoping that when Shane digs into the paperwork he'll find proof. When they set up the phony kidnappings, they needed a pipeline for their cashflow. What better way to clean off the money than to send it through a charitable foundation? You said it yourself. Catamount Foundation makes grants to family camps all over the state."

"Why didn't you speak up before?"

"Because the man behind the Catamount Foundation is an FBI assistant director. His name is Edward Colt."

Cal whistled. "What tipped you off?"

"Good Sam. The bank robber we've been looking for all this time. Her name is Shelly Catalina, formerly with the FBI. Colt doesn't know her identity. He's been using me to try to find her." She stared up the road in the direction where the trucks had disappeared. "It bothers me that the banker's body was found so close to the survivalist camp."

"It wasn't a frame-up. If it hadn't been for Wright's car accident, we wouldn't have found him."

"Whoever dumped the body didn't put it there to be close to the survivalists. They wanted it to be far away from the women. I'm starting to think that these two camps are working together."

"The target-tippers and the crystal-lovers? That seems far-fetched."

"It's perfect. Catamount's not just recycling fraud money. They're buying supplies."

"Weapons? You think this guy Colt has a private army?"

"I think he's bankrolling and arming the survivalists. And they're storing their surplus at the women's camp." She paused. "Catalina's after him. He may have had Amelia kidnapped so that, if he's cornered, he has a hostage." She opened the car door. "Go get Shane. He can do the paperwork later. Tell him to get up here."

He grabbed her arm. "Where do you think you're going?"

"To rescue Amelia Wright."

"Not by yourself."

"Cal, round up your deputies. Colt didn't pull the trigger at the hospital, but he hired someone to do it. He's responsible for Hollander's death." She could see his jaw tighten. "Stay off the radio. It's not secure. I'm going to get Amelia."

He reached under his seat. "Take a flashlight."

She kept her eyes averted until his taillights were gone. There was still some twilight left, but it was raining harder. She didn't turn on the light. She waited, letting her eyes adjust. Gradually, the shadows solidified into rocks and trees. She climbed the access road to the women's retreat.

Suni waited until she could no longer hear the trucks. Thunder echoed. The approaching storm boomed through the notch. She moved from her cover toward the sheds. Over the ridge, lightning sheeted. She flattened herself to the ground. A door at the back of the lodge opened and voices spilled out. Suni rolled behind a tree.

A plump woman hefted a set of keys. "I want to check the stores before the rain hits."

A wiry woman paused to light a cigarette. "Get me a can of pineapple for breakfast."

The big woman walked to the farthest shed. Keys jangled and the door scraped open. Only the beam of her light disappeared inside. The lock clicked back into place. She unlocked the near shed. When she backed out, she was balancing cans in each arm. The skinny form lingered, then the cigarette winked out.

Suni took a pullover from her pack. She'd insisted, to the fashion-conscious clerk, on one dark shirt. Her second shopping trip had been to a hardware store. Bolt-cutters came out of the pack. Running between fingers of lightning, she reached the nearest shed. The padlock snapped and her light passed over canned fruit, bags of onions and potatoes. She pushed the door shut and left the lock dangling. The second shed was deeper in the woods. The lock gave way, and Suni stepped into waterproof, airtight darkness.

Amelia struggled, tormented by remnants of nightmare. But she wasn't dreaming. She still felt the doctor's weight, still saw the spreading stain. She'd been awake for the horror then, and she was awake for it now. She lay on her side, breathing shallowly through her nose. A swatch of tape prevented air from entering her mouth and trapped screams in her throat. More tape wrapped her wrists and ankles. Her head was pounding and her skin itched, an irritating sensation that finally penetrated through pain. Slowly, she pushed herself up. Her hands were behind her, legs straight out in front. She couldn't see. At her back, she felt wood, and something softer, scratchy, underneath. Wool. She was sitting on a blanket. And she was naked. Fear turned to rage. She thrashed and bucked until she toppled sideways. Nausea wrenched her stomach and bolts of headache threatened to split her skull. Bile rose. Terrified, she lay still and sucked air through her nose, willed herself not to vomit. She lay as she'd fallen, curled into herself, and tried not to feel anything at all.

A light came and went. She thought she'd dreamed it. After a while, she saw another light and heard a voice from a different nightmare.

"I'll help you." The light was behind her. She struggled to sit up. "Hold still. I'll help, I promise."

I promise. Broken and raped, lying in a wet alley, she'd heard those words. She flinched as something cold touched her skin.

"Lie still. I'm going to cut the tape." Her hands came free. "This will hurt." The tape was yanked from her lips. The light clicked off and she felt movement in front of her. Hands touched her legs, cut the bindings. "Are you okay?"

As soon as she was free, Amelia launched herself toward the voice.

Suni fell back, grappling with Amelia. She tried to catch the pummeling fists. "Stop it. Amelia, stop, it's me, Suni." She grunted as the punches continued.

She thrust her knee between Amelia's legs, caught her shoulders and twisted. They rolled. Suni pinned her. She'd seen that she was naked, but feeling Amelia's body beneath her was a shock.

Amelia stopped struggling. "Suni? Is it really you?" Her arms and legs were trembling.

"Yeah."

"It was you in Boston. You killed him."

"Yes."

"I don't understand."

"Let me get you some clothes. Don't hit me anymore."

"My head hurts too much." In the flashlight beam, pink and black spandex looked garish. Amelia pulled on tights and a windbreaker, then slumped against a crate. "You're the Good Sam shooter. You killed the man who raped me."

"You never should have been involved in this. I'm sorry."

Amelia tried to stand and winced. Suni moved to help her.

"Get away from me," she hissed. "Don't touch me."

"Amelia —"

"You fucking liar."

Suni sighed. "You know me better than most people, Amelia. You know the side of me that's worth knowing. The rest of it — I used to work for the FBI. I'd show you my credentials, but I resigned when I got . . . disillusioned. They know me by my American name. Shelly Catalina." She smiled. "If you ever go sailing again, go to the Catalina Islands. Better yet, go to Thailand. I think you'd like it."

Amelia said angrily, "If you worked for the FBI, then why were they tormenting me to find you?"

"I robbed some banks. They thought you saw me."

"I didn't."

"Even I wasn't sure, until we went sailing."

Amelia's voice was colder than winter seawater. "Is this how you get your kicks, Suni? Or is it Shelly? Catalina." She spat the name. "Which did you enjoy more — fucking my body or my mind?"

"I wasn't lying when I made love to you."

Silence stretched.

Amelia asked, "How much does June know?"

"She should know who I am by now. Gavin's being used. They tried to set her up for the bank robberies."

"The FBI thinks June's involved?"

"They wanted it to look that way. Somebody has to take a fall. Why not Gavin?"

Amelia lunged. Her fist caught Suni in the gut. Suni slammed her against a crate. "Stop it! Gavin won't hang. I took care of it."

Amelia's face went pale but her voice was steady. "Let go."

"Not until I get you out of here."

She threw off Suni's hands and looked around. "Where are we?"

"In a storage shed at Sunset Ridge. You have to get out of here. With any luck, Gavin will be looking for you."

"Good." Amelia crossed her arms. "We'll wait."

"You don't understand —" Suni gripped her shoulders.

"Let go of me."

Suni pushed her roughly aside. She yanked a screwdriver from her pack and pried the lid off a crate. "Take a look." She passed her light over the open box.

Amelia stared. "Why is a camp full of lentil-eaters collecting assault weapons?"

"The camp itself is legitimate. But the people running it are crooks, and the money funding it is dirty." She began prying open crates, heaving the lids off. In the last row, farthest from the door, she had to use the bolt-cutters to sever a padlock.

Amelia gasped. "Is that —?"

"Gold." Suni nodded. "I knew there had to be more money here. He was moving it out of the banks. I guess he didn't like his NOW account."

"Does the FBI know?"

"That's the whole point. One man in the FBI's behind it. I gave Gavin the numbers. By tomorrow, it'll be public record."

Amelia said caustically, "What did you do with your share of the take?"

"I stole as much of his money as I could get. I bought my boats. I also made a large donation to a women's health center in San Francisco. Anonymously."

"What's with the one-woman vigilante act? If you know who's behind it, turn him in."

Suni hesitated. "It's personal." She said, "You're not safe here, Amelia. Get out now."

She dug into her pack and removed a wrapped bundle. She placed it beside the crates and moved deeper into the shed. Several more bundles came out of the pack. She spaced them between the rows.

"What are you doing?" Amelia was following her.

"Laying dynamite. It's easy to get in Mexico, especially if you speak the language."

"You can't do this."

Suni said, "I don't really care about the guns. Or the gold." She faced Amelia. "I've never met the man who's responsible for all of this. But I placed a lot of faith in him. So you can imagine how I felt when I realized I'd have to destroy him."

"You're insane. You're going to blow up a camp full of women. I won't let you."

"This doesn't concern you anymore."

Amelia backed up until she was braced against the door. "Neither one of us leaves this shed. Not until June Gavin gets here."

Once more, Suni reached into her pack. The gun in her hand was a revolver. Nothing automatic, nothing fancy. Working in the Bureau's computer labs, she hadn't needed a weapon. When she quit the Bureau, she got the revolver, then she began tracking Colt for a different reason — not to befriend him, but to hurt him. Two months ago, in an alley behind the bank, she'd fired a shot and then knelt to help the woman on the ground. Standing in the mountain shed, she aimed again. She pointed the gun at Amelia.

Amelia couldn't retreat any farther. "You already saved my life. You're not going to shoot me now."

"Run, Amelia." Suni reached past her and pushed open the door. "Warn the women. Tell them to get off the mountain. It's going to burn."

For a moment, Suni touched her. Amelia felt the hard muzzle of the revolver. She stumbled backward. Outside, a storm was in full fury. Wind roared and tore at tree branches. Lightning flashed earthward and thunder hammered after it. She ran and tripped, grabbed a tree and pulled herself upright. She looked back. Lightning flared. She saw Suni, arm raised, taking aim. Thunder boomed as the shed exploded. Amelia ran, and rain pounded after her.

Chapter 17

At the top of the trail, a bobbing light circled. A string of lights came parading downhill.

"Stay in line. Keep moving."

June recognized the scruffy voice. "Skinny! What happened?"

Skinny wore a rain slicker, yellow sleeves pushed to the elbow. Her flashlight made a distorted arc as women filed past. "Sixteen, seventeen, eighteen. Okay, that's everyone. No — where's Wanda?"

June had to yell to make herself heard. "What happened?"

"Lightning hit a shed. I can't find Wanda."

June pushed her toward the access road. "Get those women down. I'll find her."

Jagged light illuminated the fear on Skinny's face. "She won't leave. I have to go back."

June pointed to the straggling group. The line wavered, broke apart. "They need your help. Get them down." She forced her flashlight into Skinny's hand. "I'll go for Wanda."

Skinny's gruff voice carried briefly. "Stay in line. Stay calm. Keep moving." The wind drowned her words.

June raced up the path. She gulped air and smelled smoke. As she crested the trail, she saw the flames. One of the sheds was consumed; fire licked the surrounding trees. Wood hissed and pine needles shivered. Moisture-laden branches scorched but didn't ignite. Around the lodge, the dirt path formed a natural fire-break. The flames bent in on themselves, hot and furious.

June ran toward the lodge, toward the fire extinguishers in the kitchen. She was almost at the back door when it burst open. Electric light dribbled out, sickly yellow against the robust flames. Wanda was in the doorway. On a chain around her neck, her glasses reflected fire. The cat's head on her sweat-shirt snarled.

June ducked aside as Wanda rushed past. Wanda carried a shovel, running straight for the shed. "Wanda, no!" June sprinted after her and was driven back by the heat. The splintered door was unhinged, skewed across the entrance. Flames lapped around, beneath it. The shovel raised. June screamed, "No!" Heat seared her skin.

The shovel crashed down. Pulverized, the door collapsed. Through the maw, the storm howled in. June threw up a hand to block the heat. The last explosion came from deep in the shed. From the cavity, splinters like pine needles spewed, followed by a mouthful of flame. Heat engulfed her; June hit the ground and rolled. Wanda shrieked as fire clawed her body. She ran, still waving the shovel. Flames lapped along her arms, and her torso became an inferno. She fell to her knees. Her head ignited last.

June was on her feet. Her nerve endings screeched an alarm but the fire sucked her closer. Flames glistened. Raindrops burst. June stared, mesmerized, as the fire cast a halo. For an instant, terror faded. Captivated, she opened her mouth. And tried to breathe. Immediately, heat parched her throat. She choked; tears streamed from her eyes. She stumbled forward.

Wanda had fallen. June threw herself on the half-human, half-cooked body and crushed what was left of the flames. Then hands were on her shoulders. She resisted; someone pushed hard and tumbled her off. Wanda's blackened figure was dragged clear of the heat. June got to her knees, coughing. She heard a crash, and what was left of the shed caved in. Water beat mercilessly on the gutted remains.

Wanda lay face down. June crawled to her, tugged a hip and shoulder until she rolled. Eyes bulged like popped eggs, white and runny. Flesh dripped from finger bones. The sweatshirt and logo were gone, the fabric melted. Charred threads were embedded in burnt skin. Where the snarling catamount had been, the chest moved. Yellow teeth cracked open and breath rattled. Then the life signs disintegrated.

June clambered to her feet and turned. She reached for her Browning.

A woman's voice said, "Don't." A revolver was cocked, the barrel aimed at Amelia.

Slowly, June dropped her hand. "Catalina."

"Agent Gavin. Did you find my disk?"

"Let go of Amelia. Then we'll talk."

"Sorry, Gavin. You're not negotiating this one." She had one hand wrapped around Amelia's arm. The gun was pointing at her neck. Oddly, Amelia looked calm.

"She's bluffing," Amelia said. "She won't shoot me. Did the campers get down?"

"Yes. Catalina, let her go."

"Answer me. Did you get the data off the disk?"

"The numbers are being checked by my supervisor, Shane Isaacs. What are you going to do, Catalina?"

"Call me Suni. It's the name I grew up with in Thailand."

"How did you get those numbers?"

"When I was working for the Bureau, I spent a lot of time digging through private files, unearthing personal information. It took me a while to figure out how all that income was being generated, and where it was going. Did you find the Catamount Foundation?"

"Isaacs is investigating. We'll need your statement."

"Look for Colt. He's under a lot of layers, but he's there."

From the direction of the access road, June heard sirens. "I'm going to take you into custody, Catalina. The charge is bank robbery."

Amelia tried to tug free, but the grip on her arm tightened. June's muscles twitched. She moved imperceptibly closer. The fierce rain had abated. The air was full of misty drizzle.

Catalina said, "I can't stay to make a formal statement. You were right, Amelia. I wouldn't shoot you." Without warning, she pushed her. Off-balance, Amelia stumbled against June. Then Catalina was running through the woods.

June began to sprint but Amelia caught her. "Don't shoot her."

"Let go." She shook herself free.

Amelia clutched her. "She saved my life."

Amelia heard the clamor of sirens and watched as Suni dashed into the woods. June, gun in hand, was prepared to give chase.

She held her back. "Don't." The sirens sounded closer.

June tried to pull away.

For a long time, in the alley, there were no sirens, only terror, and pain. Then finally, a voice. "I'll help. I promise."

Amelia held onto June with all her strength.

When the lights and men swarmed into the camp, she found herself shoved into a thick, uniformed chest.

June said, "Hold her, Cal."

Then June's form became another shadow in the forest.

* * * * *

Suni squinted through the darkness. A flashlight beam bounced off the trees, then hovered on the trail. She crept closer, moving slowly toward the light until she could see his face. He was stalking, crouched low, like a fat hound on scent. In his file picture, he looked younger, less paunchy. She wondered if he'd seen Wanda's body yet. He and his wife had just celebrated their thirtieth class reunion.

She stepped onto the path behind him and raised her gun. "Colt." He began to swing around. "Don't turn."

He said, "Let me see who you are."

"Drop your gun."

He held his arms stiffly, his gun and flashlight pointing down. "Is that you, Good Sam? Are you the hacker who's been stealing my money?"

"Call me Suni. That's what my mother used to call me. You knew her a long time ago. In Thailand."

He grunted. "What do you want with me?"

"Nothing. Just to see you. Just to let you hear my voice. You and your wife didn't have children. I thought you might be ... interested."

"Why should I be? You're the child of a whore."

"She wasn't a whore when you fell in love with her. Only after you abandoned her."

"I got transferred. I told her I'd come back."

"You got her pregnant and her family kicked her out. Then you came back to the States and married your old high school sweetheart. My mother sent me to find you. I wanted to know you, Colt. I wanted to be like you. You worked for the Bureau, so I joined, too. Before I met you, I wanted to find out everything about you. I understand the Catamount

Foundation. I know what money means. But why guns, Colt? Why do you want the guns?"

"I thought I could help this country." He turned his head, spat. "It used to be worth fighting for. I used to care about protecting it. Now I protect my family and my property."

"Wanda's dead." He flinched. "I'm your family."

His voice was low. "I didn't abandon your mother. I went back for her."

"But you didn't want her."

He gave a harsh laugh. "I loved her country." His voice shook. "I fell in love with it. But she betrayed me. She showed me who she really was — a prostitute with a squalid brat. My country's better off without whores like her. And you. You're not mine."

"Look at me before you disown me."

He began to turn. "I'll kill you for what you cost me."

June spotted the light, then Colt and Catalina. They were at the front of the camp, close to the ridge trail. The lights and commotion of the sheriff's men were behind her.

She stepped cautiously into the clearing. Catalina had her gun on Colt.

June aimed the Browning. "Catalina. You're covered. Drop it." She called, "We know about the Catamount Foundation, Colt. Surrender your weapon and turn yourself in."

Colt's hand jerked up. "Gavin?" He aimed his

heavy double-action pistol at June. Catalina's revolver stayed trained on him. "Shoot her," he snarled.

June kept her sights on Catalina. They were three points of a triangle, connected by the lines between targets and guns.

She said, "Catalina, do as I say. Drop your weapon."

Colt's flashlight searched June's face, momentarily blinding her. She blinked. For a split second, she pulled her gaze from Catalina to Colt.

"No way are you taking me down, Gavin." His light wavered. Her eyes focused and she saw his grip tighten.

Her Browning was still aimed at Catalina. She knew Colt was going to shoot her, and she knew she didn't have time to change her target.

She dove to the ground, but a gunshot had already resounded.

She rolled and came up. Catalina was standing over Colt. June moved forward. He was sprawled, his gun hand limp, fingers slack, the flashlight trapped beneath him. Catalina prodded him and the flashlight rolled out. His ring finger poked into the light, the garish jewel glinting, the cat's head frozen in gold.

The sound of the shot had drawn the sheriff's men toward the front clearing. She didn't wait. Catalina had already taken off down the trail. June sprinted after her.

A few hundred meters above the turnout, Catalina stopped and looked back. She shut her light and remained still, letting June come toward her. June picked her way down, gun steady, her aim never wavering. Catalina unzipped her pack and put away her gun. June closed to twenty meters.

"I'm leaving the country," Catalina called. June couldn't be sure, but she thought Catalina was smiling. "You were going to shoot me, weren't you?"

"I should have stopped you from firing on Colt. I wasn't fast enough."

"I'm going to Thailand. Please tell Amelia I said good-bye."

Mist swirled and lifted. For a moment, June could see her clearly — a tiny woman on a wet mountain-side. She engaged her safety. She stared a minute longer, then holstered her gun. "Have a safe trip." She turned and hiked back to the lodge.

The sheriff's men met her at the top of the trail. A light splashed over her. "Anyone down there?"

"It's clear to the turnout."

The light was in her face. "You go all the way down?"

"Yeah." She closed her eyes. "It's clear."

"All right, let's go. Take it around the other side." The lights and shouting moved off.

Catalina had a chance. Cal would radio a description to his deputies, but there were a lot of trails. With Colt injured or dead, there was going to be a lot of confusion. June gave her even odds.

Amelia was sitting on the lodge steps. A gauze bandage wrapped one foot.

"Are you hurt?"

"My feet got cut up. The sheriff made one of his Cub Scouts apply direct pressure."

June took her hand. "Come on. I'll take you home."

Chapter 18

The Fourth of July party had been Marj's idea.

"It's the only time all summer I've been to the beach," she complained cheerfully.

"That's because you spend every vacation moment in the mountains," Amelia said.

Dr. Rachel Saks appeared on the porch, a cane in one hand, a tray of vegetables in the other. "Marj, honey, where do you want this?"

Marj was directing BJ and Amelia to set up a folding table. "Don't move. I'll get it." Rachel descended the steps. "Be careful," Marj scolded. "Come sit down. I'll start the water boiling."

BJ took the vegetable tray. "Please don't boil water."

Marj gestured to the barbecue. "Grill yourself some tofu. The rest of us are eating lobster."

He helped Rachel to a chair. "You're a doctor. Can't you do something about the way she eats?"

"She nursed me back to health on a steady diet of danish. She's doing something right."

Marj placed a protective hand on Rachel's shoulder. "Leave her alone, or you'll find yourself camel-packing in the Sahara."

Rachel covered Marj's hand. "I have a little influence, BJ. I'll keep her healthy."

Amelia turned away from the tenderness. Her new red Jeep was parked at the curb. As she watched, a dark blue Porsche snugged up behind it. June Gavin helped a regal, silver-haired woman from the car. BJ greeted them at the gate.

"BJ, I'd like you to meet Gretchen Jensen."

"June tells me you make your own beer." Her voice was beautiful, melodious.

June said, "Go get some ginseng, BJ."

He offered Gretchen his arm. "I'm experimenting with different flavors. Do you like raspberries?"

"I adore raspberries."

She waited for June to approach her.

"Marj invited us," June said.

"I know. It's about time you got here. Come on, let's take a walk." When they were out of sight of the cottage, she dropped to the sand. June sat down, keeping a little space between them. "You've been a stranger," Amelia said.

"Things have been busy at work. And after what happened with Bryanna, I thought you might need a little time."

Amelia watched the waves. "How'd you know it was her?"

"All those logging roads. I checked the map a dozen times. You can drive from one side of that mountain to the other in less than an hour." June wasn't wearing sunglasses. In the light, her eyes shone like teak. "While I was looking for you, one of the sheriff's men was checking Littleton motels. When he found her, the receipt from a cheap six-pack was still in her wallet."

The breeze tumbled Amelia's hair into her eyes and she brushed it back. That night at the sheriff's station, she'd glimpsed June, still wet and sooty from the mountain ordeal, escorting Bryanna into an interrogation room. She imagined her, damp and fearsome, terrifying Bryanna into a tearful confession.

"You suspected her all along, didn't you?"

"Catalina would have killed you earlier, if you'd been a threat, and Colt didn't have you abducted until after the Jeep accident. He didn't want to push you off the mountain. He needed a hostage."

"I wouldn't share her candy, so Bryanna bashed me on the head. It was stupid of her to use beer. She knows I don't drink."

"The rescue squad didn't know. Until Rachel did a blood level, everyone assumed it was drunk driving."

Amelia said angrily, "What was she thinking? Attack me, wait a day or two, then come kiss my bruises?"

"Seems like she always liked you better as an invalid."

Amelia shuddered. "There's some kind of flyer circulating for the Bryanna Waters' Defense Fund. Spare me."

"She was charged in New Hampshire with second degree assault and reckless conduct. Even if her lawyer negotiates a plea, she'll probably serve six months to a year."

"That's not long enough."

"When New Hampshire's done with her, she's facing a penalty for the handgun violation in Massachusetts. That charge carries up to a year's imprisonment."

"I have a restraining order. If she comes near me, I'll —"

"You'll what?" June shifted closer.

"You'll think of something." Their shoulders were touching. "What's going on with the feds?"

"There was a shake-up. And a cover-up. With Colt dead, it was easier to contain. Our press department worked overtime on that." She smiled. "Shane took Marj to a very expensive restaurant. She really helped break open the Catamount Foundation. I think he was disappointed when she got serious with Rachel."

"Marj loved playing special agent. You made her very happy."

"There's been a lot of buzz about the Bureau's computers. They couldn't find any evidence that Colt was setting me up, but the systems analyst who was working for him, a guy named Al Rahman, took an early retirement."

"Sunset Ridge Retreat closed down," Amelia said. "Imagine my dismay when I had to leave it out of my article on rock climbing."

June chuckled. "The sheriff said the survivalists have cleared out, too, but they'll probably resurface later, somewhere else."

"Is the FBI going after Suni?"

"They had to do a lot of damage control around Colt. I don't think they want to stir things up with an international search. As long as she's out of the country, she's safe."

Amelia mused, "Maybe I'll pick up some freelance work. I could do a piece on sailing in Southeast Asia." She studied June. "You let her go, didn't you?"

"That's not what I told my supervisor."

"Does it bother you — the decision you made?"

"It's not keeping me awake at night." June stretched her legs. "How's the head?"

"No more dizziness or nausea. I still get headaches, but I blame them on Marj." She hesitated. "I don't get the flashbacks as much."

"That's a good sign." June turned slightly. "You've put on some weight. You look good."

"I installed a new sound system in the cottage. I thought Elvis Costello might help my cooking. Great music, but my lasagna's a disaster."

"Sounds like I should start coming around."

"Don't bring the landlady."

"I'll take her to BJ's. Do you think he likes opera?"

"He loves opera."

June smiled. "Do you eat clams? An old buddy of mine keeps badgering me to get together. I'd like him to meet you. His name is Bass."

"Like the fish?"

"You got it."

Amelia let herself relax. Beside her, June was

dressed in shorts and a soft white jersey. Comfortable. Still not enough color. Amelia kicked off her shoes and dug her toes into the sand. It was warm on the surface, cool underneath. She moved her foot, pressed it against June's leg.

"You'd better start talking. I'll make you a deal. First you tell me your story, the whole unedited version. If I like it, I'll take you to bed."

June asked, "Is that how it works? I guess that sounds fair."

June's body blocked the sun but rays of heat escaped, outlining the long nose, the curved lips. Amelia touched her, softness and sunlight. Then all she felt was June's rock-solid embrace.

They strolled back to the cottage, holding hands.

BJ beamed as they walked through the gate. He said to June, "The barbarians are boiling live crustaceans. Will you join me for a veggie burger?"

"Sure, BJ." She whispered to Amelia, "Can I have a bite of your lobster?"

Amelia grinned. "I'll go tell Marj to save us a big one."

BJ gave June a measured look. "She talks to you, doesn't she?"

June smiled. "We take turns."

"BJ!" Marj hollered from the porch. "Get those beautiful muscles up here and into my kitchen."

June sat with Gretchen and Rachel on the patio.

The doctor took her hands. "I heard you got

burned." She stroked a thumb across the palm. "It looks like the skin's healed nicely."

"I'm fine. How are you, Rachel?"

"A little stiffer than I used to be." Her eyes crinkled. "Falling in love takes some of the sting out."

June pressed her hand. "You did good, Doc."

Rachel met her eyes. "I heard the stories. Sounds like there was quite a fire."

"It didn't spread, and the rain put it out pretty fast."

"Any extra-visual side effects?"

She remembered the fire — the way the colors had danced, cajoled. She felt the buffeting flames. She remembered gulping air, and how the heat had scorched her throat. She smelled charred wood and flesh, the odors soaking into her clothes like rain. She remembered Wanda's body, and the searing pain when they'd lain, for a moment, connected by fire.

She said, "No hallucinations. Just the dreams. But they don't scare me as much." Amelia came to sit beside her. "My reputation at the Bureau is pretty well trashed. They wanted to know why I never took out Catalina. I tried to explain that Colt's light was in my eyes. So they changed my nickname. Instead of sure-shot, I'm blind-spot."

Rachel laughed. "Do you think you can live without the heroics?"

Amelia said, "I won't let her get bored. Have you ever been sky diving? I think parachutes come in every color but navy blue."

June clasped her hand. Over the ocean, sunlight

splashed on endless waves. Summer heat sank into her shoulders. Inside, everything stilled, like the lull in a breeze.

Amelia's lips touched her. "Do you think she made it?"

June kissed her lightly. "Yes. I do."

Beyond the horizon, wind rushed to meet the waves, and an orange and black hull raced across blue ocean. Suni squinted at the sun and tacked into the wind. The sailboat heeled. Muscles strained, sails strained, and over the bow, wind raged and water shattered.

A few of the publications of
THE NAIAD PRESS, INC.
P.O. Box 10543 • Tallahassee, Florida 32302
Phone (850) 539-5965
Toll-Free Order Number: 1-800-533-1973
Mail orders welcome. Please include 15% postage.
Write or call for our free catalog which also features an
incredible selection of lesbian videos.

SEA TO SHINING SEA by Lisa Shapiro. 256 pp. Unable to resist
the raging passion . . .   ISBN 1-56280-177-5 $11.95

THIRD DEGREE by Kate Calloway. 224 pp. 3rd Cassidy James
mystery.   ISBN 1-56280-185-6   11.95

WHEN THE DANCING STOPS by Therese Szymanski. 272 pp.
1st Brett Higgins mystery.   ISBN 1-56280-186-4   11.95

PHASES OF THE MOON by Julia Watts. 192 pp. . . . . . hungry
for everything life has to offer.   ISBN 1-56280-176-7   11.95

BABY IT'S COLD by Jaye Maiman. 256 pp. 5th Robin Miller
mystery.   ISBN 1-56280-156-2   10.95

CLASS REUNION by Linda Hill. 176 pp. The girl from her past . . .
                                                 ISBN 1-56280-178-3   11.95

DREAM LOVER by Lyn Denison. 224 pp. A soft, sensuous,
romantic fantasy.   ISBN 1-56280-173-1   11.95

FORTY LOVE by Diana Simmonds. 288 pp. Joyous, heart-
warming romance.   ISBN 1-56280-171-6   11.95

IN THE MOOD by Robbi Sommers. 160 pp. The queen of
erotic tension!   ISBN 1-56280-172-4   11.95

SWIMMING CAT COVE by Lauren Douglas. 192 pp. 2nd
Allison O'Neil Mystery.   ISBN 1-56280-168-6   11.95

THE LOVING LESBIAN by Claire McNab and Sharon Gedan.
240 pp. Explore the experiences that make lesbian love unique.
                                                 ISBN 1-56280-169-4   14.95

COURTED by Celia Cohen. 160 pp. Sparkling romantic
encounter.   ISBN 1-56280-166-X   11.95

SEASONS OF THE HEART by Jackie Calhoun. 240 pp. Romance
through the years.   ISBN 1-56280-167-8   11.95

K. C. BOMBER by Janet McClellan. 208 pp. 1st Tru North
mystery.   ISBN 1-56280-157-0   11.95

NOW AND THEN by Penny Hayes. 240 pp. Romance on the
westward journey.   ISBN 1-56280-121-X   11.95

HEART ON FIRE by Diana Simmonds. 176 pp. The romantic and
erotic rival of *Curious Wine*.   ISBN 1-56280-152-X   11.95

DEATH AT LAVENDER BAY by Lauren Wright Douglas. 208 pp.
1st Allison O'Neil Mystery.   ISBN 1-56280-085-X   11.95

YES I SAID YES I WILL by Judith McDaniel. 272 pp. Hot
romance by famous author.   ISBN 1-56280-138-4   11.95

FORBIDDEN FIRES by Margaret C. Anderson. Edited by Mathilda
Hills. 176 pp. Famous author's "unpublished" Lesbian romance.
                                      ISBN 1-56280-123-6   21.95

SIDE TRACKS by Teresa Stores. 160 pp. Gender-bending
Lesbians on the road.   ISBN 1-56280-122-8   10.95

HOODED MURDER by Annette Van Dyke. 176 pp. 1st Jessie
Batelle Mystery.   ISBN 1-56280-134-1   10.95

WILDWOOD FLOWERS by Julia Watts. 208 pp. Hilarious and
heart-warming tale of true love.   ISBN 1-56280-127-9   10.95

NEVER SAY NEVER by Linda Hill. 224 pp. Rule #1: Never get involved
with . . .   ISBN 1-56280-126-0   10.95

THE SEARCH by Melanie McAllester. 240 pp. Exciting top cop
Tenny Mendoza case.   ISBN 1-56280-150-3   10.95

THE WISH LIST by Saxon Bennett. 192 pp. Romance through
the years.   ISBN 1-56280-125-2   10.95

FIRST IMPRESSIONS by Kate Calloway. 208 pp. P.I. Cassidy
James' first case.   ISBN 1-56280-133-3   10.95

OUT OF THE NIGHT by Kris Bruyer. 192 pp. Spine-tingling
thriller.   ISBN 1-56280-120-1   10.95

NORTHERN BLUE by Tracey Richardson. 224 pp. Police recruits
Miki & Miranda — passion in the line of fire. ISBN 1-56280-118-X   10.95

LOVE'S HARVEST by Peggy J. Herring. 176 pp. by the author of
Once More With Feeling.   ISBN 1-56280-117-1   10.95

THE COLOR OF WINTER by Lisa Shapiro. 208 pp. Romantic
love beyond your wildest dreams.   ISBN 1-56280-116-3   10.95

FAMILY SECRETS by Laura DeHart Young. 208 pp. Enthralling
romance and suspense.   ISBN 1-56280-119-8   10.95

INLAND PASSAGE by Jane Rule. 288 pp. Tales exploring conven-
tional & unconventional relationships.   ISBN 0-930044-56-8   10.95

DOUBLE BLUFF by Claire McNab. 208 pp. 7th Carol Ashton
Mystery.   ISBN 1-56280-096-5   10.95

BAR GIRLS by Lauran Hoffman. 176 pp. See the movie, read
the book!   ISBN 1-56280-115-5   10.95

THE FIRST TIME EVER edited by Barbara Grier & Christine Cassidy. 272 pp. Love stories by Naiad Press authors.
ISBN 1-56280-086-8   14.95

MISS PETTIBONE AND MISS McGRAW by Brenda Weathers. 208 pp. A charming ghostly love story.   ISBN 1-56280-151-1   10.95

CHANGES by Jackie Calhoun. 208 pp. Involved romance and relationships.   ISBN 1-56280-083-3   10.95

FAIR PLAY by Rose Beecham. 256 pp. 3rd Amanda Valentine Mystery.   ISBN 1-56280-081-7   10.95

PAYBACK by Celia Cohen. 176 pp. A gripping thriller of romance, revenge and betrayal.   ISBN 1-56280-084-1   10.95

THE BEACH AFFAIR by Barbara Johnson. 224 pp. Sizzling summer romance/mystery/intrigue.   ISBN 1-56280-090-6   10.95

GETTING THERE by Robbi Sommers. 192 pp. Nobody does it like Robbi!   ISBN 1-56280-099-X   10.95

FINAL CUT by Lisa Haddock. 208 pp. 2nd Carmen Ramirez Mystery.   ISBN 1-56280-088-4   10.95

FLASHPOINT by Katherine V. Forrest. 256 pp. A Lesbian blockbuster!   ISBN 1-56280-079-5   10.95

CLAIRE OF THE MOON by Nicole Conn. Audio Book —Read by Marianne Hyatt.   ISBN 1-56280-113-9   16.95

FOR LOVE AND FOR LIFE: INTIMATE PORTRAITS OF LESBIAN COUPLES by Susan Johnson. 224 pp.
ISBN 1-56280-091-4   14.95

DEVOTION by Mindy Kaplan. 192 pp. See the movie — read the book!   ISBN 1-56280-093-0   10.95

SOMEONE TO WATCH by Jaye Maiman. 272 pp. 4th Robin Miller Mystery.   ISBN 1-56280-095-7   10.95

GREENER THAN GRASS by Jennifer Fulton. 208 pp. A young woman — a stranger in her bed.   ISBN 1-56280-092-2   10.95

TRAVELS WITH DIANA HUNTER by Regine Sands. Erotic lesbian romp. Audio Book (2 cassettes)   ISBN 1-56280-107-4   16.95

CABIN FEVER by Carol Schmidt. 256 pp. Sizzling suspense and passion.   ISBN 1-56280-089-1   10.95

THERE WILL BE NO GOODBYES by Laura DeHart Young. 192 pp. Romantic love, strength, and friendship.   ISBN 1-56280-103-1   10.95

FAULTLINE by Sheila Ortiz Taylor. 144 pp. Joyous comic lesbian novel.   ISBN 1-56280-108-2   9.95

OPEN HOUSE by Pat Welch. 176 pp. 4th Helen Black Mystery.
ISBN 1-56280-102-3   10.95

ONCE MORE WITH FEELING by Peggy J. Herring. 240 pp. Lighthearted, loving romantic adventure.   ISBN 1-56280-089-2   10.95

FOREVER by Evelyn Kennedy. 224 pp. Passionate romance — love overcoming all obstacles.   ISBN 1-56280-094-9   10.95

WHISPERS by Kris Bruyer. 176 pp. Romantic ghost story
                                              ISBN 1-56280-082-5   10.95

NIGHT SONGS by Penny Mickelbury. 224 pp. 2nd Gianna Maglione Mystery.   ISBN 1-56280-097-3   10.95

GETTING TO THE POINT by Teresa Stores. 256 pp. Classic southern Lesbian novel.   ISBN 1-56280-100-7   10.95

PAINTED MOON by Karin Kallmaker. 224 pp. Delicious Kallmaker romance.   ISBN 1-56280-075-2   11.95

THE MYSTERIOUS NAIAD edited by Katherine V. Forrest & Barbara Grier. 320 pp. Love stories by Naiad Press authors.
                                              ISBN 1-56280-074-4   14.95

DAUGHTERS OF A CORAL DAWN by Katherine V. Forrest. 240 pp. Tenth Anniversay Edition.   ISBN 1-56280-104-X   11.95

BODY GUARD by Claire McNab. 208 pp. 6th Carol Ashton Mystery.   ISBN 1-56280-073-6   11.95

CACTUS LOVE by Lee Lynch. 192 pp. Stories by the beloved storyteller.   ISBN 1-56280-071-X   9.95

SECOND GUESS by Rose Beecham. 216 pp. 2nd Amanda Valentine Mystery.   ISBN 1-56280-069-8   9.95

A RAGE OF MAIDENS by Lauren Wright Douglas. 240 pp. 6th Caitlin Reece Mystery.   ISBN 1-56280-068-X   10.95

TRIPLE EXPOSURE by Jackie Calhoun. 224 pp. Romantic drama involving many characters.   ISBN 1-56280-067-1   10.95

UP, UP AND AWAY by Catherine Ennis. 192 pp. Delightful romance.   ISBN 1-56280-065-5   11.95

PERSONAL ADS by Robbi Sommers. 176 pp. Sizzling short stories.   ISBN 1-56280-059-0   11.95

CROSSWORDS by Penny Sumner. 256 pp. 2nd Victoria Cross Mystery.   ISBN 1-56280-064-7   9.95

SWEET CHERRY WINE by Carol Schmidt. 224 pp. A novel of suspense.   ISBN 1-56280-063-9   9.95

CERTAIN SMILES by Dorothy Tell. 160 pp. Erotic short stories.
                                              ISBN 1-56280-066-3   9.95

EDITED OUT by Lisa Haddock. 224 pp. 1st Carmen Ramirez Mystery.   ISBN 1-56280-077-9   9.95

WEDNESDAY NIGHTS by Camarin Grae. 288 pp. Sexy adventure.   ISBN 1-56280-060-4   10.95

SMOKEY O by Celia Cohen. 176 pp. Relationships on the playing field.   ISBN 1-56280-057-4   9.95

KATHLEEN O'DONALD by Penny Hayes. 256 pp. Rose and
Kathleen find each other and employment in 1909 NYC.
ISBN 1-56280-070-1   9.95

STAYING HOME by Elisabeth Nonas. 256 pp. Molly and Alix
want a baby . . . or do they?   ISBN 1-56280-076-0   10.95

TRUE LOVE by Jennifer Fulton. 240 pp. Six lesbians searching
for love in all the "right" places.   ISBN 1-56280-035-3   10.95

KEEPING SECRETS by Penny Mickelbury. 208 pp. 1st Gianna
Maglione Mystery.   ISBN 1-56280-052-3   9.95

THE ROMANTIC NAIAD edited by Katherine V. Forrest &
Barbara Grier. 336 pp. Love stories by Naiad Press authors.
ISBN 1-56280-054-X   14.95

UNDER MY SKIN by Jaye Maiman. 336 pp. 3rd Robin Miller
Mystery.   ISBN 1-56280-049-3.   11.95

CAR POOL by Karin Kallmaker. 272pp. Lesbians on wheels
and then some!   ISBN 1-56280-048-5   10.95

NOT TELLING MOTHER: STORIES FROM A LIFE by Diane
Salvatore. 176 pp. Her 3rd novel.   ISBN 1-56280-044-2   9.95

GOBLIN MARKET by Lauren Wright Douglas. 240pp. 5th Caitlin
Reece Mystery.   ISBN 1-56280-047-7   10.95

LONG GOODBYES by Nikki Baker. 256 pp. 3rd Virginia Kelly
Mystery.   ISBN 1-56280-042-6   9.95

FRIENDS AND LOVERS by Jackie Calhoun. 224 pp. Mid-
western Lesbian lives and loves.   ISBN 1-56280-041-8   11.95

BEHIND CLOSED DOORS by Robbi Sommers. 192 pp. Hot,
erotic short stories.   ISBN 1-56280-039-6   11.95

CLAIRE OF THE MOON by Nicole Conn. 192 pp. See the
movie — read the book!   ISBN 1-56280-038-8   10.95

SILENT HEART by Claire McNab. 192 pp. Exotic Lesbian
romance.   ISBN 1-56280-036-1   10.95

THE SPY IN QUESTION by Amanda Kyle Williams. 256 pp.
4th Madison McGuire Mystery.   ISBN 1-56280-037-X   9.95

SAVING GRACE by Jennifer Fulton. 240 pp. Adventure and
romantic entanglement.   ISBN 1-56280-051-5   10.95

These are just a few of the many Naiad Press titles — we are the oldest and
largest lesbian/feminist publishing company in the world. We also offer an
enormous selection of lesbian video products. Please request a complete
catalog. We offer personal service; we encourage and welcome direct mail
orders from individuals who have limited access to bookstores carrying our
publications.